Cruising with the O'Maras

The Irish Guesthouse on the Green, Book 17

Michelle Vernal

Copyright © 2025 Cruising with the O'Maras by Michelle Vernal

All rights reserved.

No portion of this book, Cruising with the O'Maras may be reproduced in any form without written permission from the publisher or author, except as permitted by U.S. copyright law.

Also by Michelle Vernal

♥

Novels
The Little Irish Farm (previously titled Secondhand Jane)
Staying at Eleni's
The Traveller's Daughter
Sweet Home Summer
When We Say Goodbye
And...
Series fiction
The Irish Guesthouse on the Green Series
Amazon series page http://mybook.to/TGseriespage
Book 1 - O'Mara's
Book 2 – Moira-Lisa Smile
Book 3 –What goes on Tour
Book 4 – Rosi's Regrets
Book 5 – Christmas at O'Mara's
Book 6 – A Wedding at O'Mara's
Book 7 – Maureen's Song
Book 8 – The O'Maras in LaLa Land
Book 9 – Due in March
Book 10 – A Baby at O'Mara's

Book 11 – The Housewarming
Book 12 – Rainbows over O'Mara's
Book 13 - An O'Maras Reunion
Book 14 - The O'Maras Go Greek
Book 15 Mat Magic at O'Mara's
Book 16 Matchmaking at O'Mara's
Book 18 Coming in 2025

Liverpool Brides Series

The Autumn Posy
The Winter Posy
The Spring Posy
The Summer Posy

Isabel's Story

The Promise
The Letter

The Little Irish Village

Christmas in the Little Irish Village
New Beginnings in the Little Irish Village
A Christmas Miracle in the Little Irish Village
Secrets in the Little Irish Village
Saving Christmas in the Little Irish Village

Chapter 1

♥

Dublin, April 2003

Aisling O'Mara was perched on the edge of her bed with her legs crossed, looking like an advertisement for a day spa in her terrycloth robe. All that was missing was the glass of bubbles. 'I think Donal's after popping the question to Mammy and she's said yes. You know what she's like. She'll have put the screws on him since Bronagh and Leonard's engagement because she doesn't like being left out.' Aisling frowned, thinking about the receptionist at O'Mara's, the guesthouse overlooking St Stephen's Green here in Dublin, and the big diamond sparkler she was apt to shoving under guests' noses, and wondering how big Mammy's ring would be. Hopefully, she wouldn't waggle her fingers and break into a breathy version of 'Diamonds are a Girl's Best Friend' each time someone feigned interest in her sparkler like Bronagh. To Aisling, she sounded more like a full-time smoker than Marilyn Monroe. Her fingers worried at an annoying loose thread on her robe. It was almost as irritating as the 'Diamonds' song, and she wasn't done with the topic yet.

'Do you think she'll take his name?' Aisling loved Donal. She did, but she didn't like the idea of Mammy no longer being an O'Mara much. It was silly because she knew it wouldn't mean Mammy would have forgotten about Daddy if she did. That was hardly likely with the fruit of his loins – Patrick, the eldest and only son, Roisin, herself and Moira, the youngest – to remind her of him.

Moira shared the family apartment they'd grown up in on the top floor of the guesthouse with Aisling. They rubbed alongside one another with their other halves and off-spring because it made financial sense in the short term. Right now, she was on her knees, arse in the air, with her head buried inside Aisling's wardrobe. Her voice was muffled as she bounced back, 'She can't because then she wouldn't be an O'Mara anymore.'

Aisling thought that was a typical 'no shades of grey' Moira way of viewing things. Her sister was scanning Aisling's covetable collection of designer stilettos on the closet's bottom shelf, which hadn't been added to since Aisling became an O'Mara-Moran and her disposable income shrank with responsibilities like a mortgage and twin babies. Killer heels didn't feature much in her day-to-day mammy wear. Today was an anomaly, however, and while Aisling was in her dressing gown waiting for Moira to get on with it and be on her way, she did have a gorgeous strappy pair of Louboutin heels on her feet, a full face of makeup and her mane of reddish-gold hair was suitably fluffed.

She gave up on the loose thread and crossed her legs, twirling her ankle to admire the sparkly gorgeousness of the shoe on her right foot. 'Oh, I've missed you,' she said quietly, thinking it was grand to have an occasion to wear them again even though she'd no clue what she would wear with them. In the worst-case scenario, she'd go in her robe. At least it would be comfy. She'd begrudgingly allowed Moira to borrow a pair of shoes for the auspicious luncheon, not out of the kindness of her heart but in exchange for babysitting bonus points.

A thought occurred to Aisling. *Mammy might choose to double barrel like me.* She went by O'Mara-Moran these days,

CHAPTER 1

proud to be Quinn Moran's wife, owner of Quinn's Bistro on nearby Baggot Street, but not having wanted to relinquish the connection to her daddy's name either. 'Maureen O'Mara-McCarthy.' She sounded out what could very well be Mammy's new name, deciding that, while a mouthful, it had a ring. She repeated it slower this time.

'I heard you the first time.' Moira's voice drifted out.

'It's strange hearing their names strung together like so. Don't you think? Not in a bad way, like. Just strange. O'Mara-McCarthy, I could live with it. Jaysus Moira, are you ever coming out of there?'

'Ash, you're getting ahead of yourself. We don't know why Mammy's summoned us for lunch, but I'm taking my time. Choosing from your designer shoe collection is like being a kid in a corner shop with your pocket money and big decisions to be made as to which sweets to buy. Don't rush me.'

Moira was out of practice when it came to dressing up, too. Her former life as a legal secretary had seen her leave the guesthouse looking like a fashion plate most mornings. These days, she fancied herself more bohemian given she was mam to the toddler Kiera and a Fine Arts student.

Aisling mulled over what she'd said about her getting ahead of herself and decided her sister was wrong. 'Cop yourself on Moira: a spontaneous, slap-up meal at Beaufield Mews, which everybody knows is a popular wedding venue. Watch this space, girl, because engagements fall under that category, too, and that's what we'll be toasting this afternoon. Donal's girls Louise and Anna and their lot are invited too.'

The expense of the meal would make your eyes water, she thought, blinking, recalling how two days ago Mammy had demanded her daughters' including Roisin, who was pregnant, and their partners Quinn, Tom and Shay, along with the twins, Aoife and Connor, the toddler Kiera and school-age Noah's presence for a slap-up lunch, at one pm sharp on Sunday. She'd ordered if they had other plans then they were to change them. Aisling knew she'd have invited Patrick, Cindy and the babby Brianna if they weren't living in Los Angeles. Patrick got out of a lot of things because of that. *Sometimes, emigration was a tempting prospect,* she mused.

It was an invitation initially met with moans of, 'It's short notice' from Aisling and, after conferring with Roisin, she found she wasn't alone in this sentiment. Meanwhile, Moira had been more concerned about the financial aspect of dining out, with her first question being, 'Are you and Donal paying, Mammy? Because Tom and I are students, you know, as well as parents.' Tom was at medical school and would one day become a doctor. It was handy having a trainee doctor in the house. Sure, Aisling had presented him with a mysterious red spot on her leg just last night. She was unsure about his abilities as she'd disliked his ingrown-hair diagnosis.

However, all moans were silenced when Mammy divulged lunch was on her and Donal. Also, a table had been booked at Beaufield Mews, thanks to a cancellation at the last minute of a wedding reception. *When you think about it, it is sad,* Aisling mulled, because it likely meant the bride or the groom had cold feet, and she knew how it felt to be let down. Still, things worked out grand for her in the end, and it was far better to pull the pin before saying 'I do'.

Moira's main concern had been whether the couple had lost their deposit on the venue.

It wasn't every day you got an invitation for a family gathering at the likes of the beautiful converted old house in Stillorgan with a stellar five-star reputation. Nor was it often Mammy was tight-lipped about anything, but on the reasons behind the last-minute lunch she would not be drawn, saying all would be revealed when they were seated around the table enjoying a convivial lunch.

The O'Mara girls had burned up the phone lines tossing theories back and forth, with the hot favourite between Aisling and Roisin being an engagement. Moira was adamant it

CHAPTER 1

was purely a spontaneous celebration of Mammy and Donal's luck in having wonderful children and precious grandchildren. That or she'd decided to formally adopt Ciara with a 'C', her fashion guru who worked at a local Howth boutique near Mammy and Donal's home with its sea view. Aisling and Roisin vetoed the suggestion because Ciara was still in the bad books over the fashion faux pas, whereby the same dress had been sold to Bronagh and Mammy. The result of which was they'd twinned at a recent family christening. Nobody bothered ringing their brother, Patrick, in Los Angeles for his input, aware that all they'd get was an earful on the trials and tribulations of being a new daddy.

'Is it a miner's head-torch you're needing?' Aisling flung at her sister's arse before averting her gaze, which lit upon the latest Marian Keyes novel on her bedside table. She'd been dipping into it before bed each night and was nearly finished. 'Marian got married there, you know.'

'Marian who?'

'Keyes. You know, the author.'

'I see, a close personal friend of yours is she?'

Aisling pulled a face even though Moira couldn't see her. 'I'm just saying.'

At last, Moira popped out from the closet, a champagne cork from a bottle or, Aisling thought a tad bitchily, like a dog who'd dug up a bone as she sat back on her haunches and waved a pair of Yves Saint Laurent platforms triumphantly. 'These are perfect.' Then, getting a sly look on her face, she asked, 'Do you know who else has dined at Beaufield?'

Aisling pulled another face. 'Ah no, not Daniel?' Instantly, an image of Daniel Day-Lewis in his *The Last of the Mohicans* loin cloth, Mammy's all-time favourite film for that very reason, frolicking amongst the spring flowers in the beautiful gardens of Beaufield Mews appeared before her. 'Mammy's probably got wind he's over there in Stillorgan filming a sequel to *The Last of the Mohicans*.'

'Sure, what would he be doing making a film about a Native American tribe in a Stillorgan restaurant?'

'I don't know, do I?'

'Anyway, I'm not talking about Daniel. It's someone else.'

'Who?' Aisling felt she was walking into a trap.

'Bono!' Her sister clapped her hands delightedly, watching Aisling, who almost had an allergic reaction whenever the singer's name was mentioned, throw herself back on the bed with an anguished yelp.

Making a swift recovery, Aisling reared back up and pointed a finger at her sister. 'So, we're clear then? You will be personally responsible, student or no student, for full replacement value should you and your cloven hooves damage my Yves Saint Laurents in any way.'

'Affirmative,' Moira bounced back with a nod. Then she slapped her chest with her hand. 'Hand on heart. I will look after these beauties as though they were my child. And can I have a squirt of your Jasper Conran while I'm here? Pretty please.'

'No. And given you lost Kiera in the Tesco yesterday, I'm not feeling reassured, Moira.'

'Ah, be fair, Ash. That wasn't my fault. It was your man on the butcher's counter. He was asking for trouble, offering her the little red sausage in the first place. How was I to know she'd toddle back for seconds?'

Aisling begged to differ. It should have been obvious, but then she and her niece were on the same wavelength regarding food. *Not just food*, she thought. Kiera burst into tears whenever she saw a photograph of your Bono man, too.

Moira disappeared and left Aisling to inspect the contents of her wardrobe. She began flinging items onto the bed, her frown becoming a scowl because nothing suitable fitted since she'd had the babies. She sat down again, wondering if she really could pull off the bathrobe look.

CHAPTER 1

Moira's figure snapped back like an elastic band after giving birth to Kiera. She reappeared in the bedroom merely minutes after vacating it. 'How do I look?' She twirled her sheet of black hair, shimmering like silk. 'I feel like the old Moira. Only a new and improved version because I'm much happier now than I used to be.'

'I can see your knickers in that IBS,' Aisling muttered, unimpressed.

'It's *LBD*: little black dress, as well you know.'

'More like itsy black sheath: IBS. It's lunch, not opening night at a club in town.' Aisling was aware she sounded like their mammy and turned her attention back to the loose thread, mumbling, 'Sorry. You look gorgeous.'

'What's got up your nose then?' Moira asked, mollified.

Aisling slapped her hands down on her thighs. 'I've nothing to wear, and Mammy's bound to take photos to mark the occasion!'

'I'd offer to loan you something, but . . .' Moira shrugged. Not even she, Mouth of Ireland's South, was prepared to suggest that Aisling would only get one leg in anything she owned. Instead, she was proactive in inspecting the contents of Aisling's wardrobe. 'Here, put this on. You look well in that shade of blue.'

'Not funny.' Aisling glowered at her sister, holding up the dress she and her sisters had nicknamed 'The Chinese Silk Prostitute Dress' because your redhead who was in *China Beach* on the tele wore something similar. Mammy had brought it back along with different colours for Moira and Rosi from her and Moira's Vietnam travels.

Then, a flash of green caught Aisling's eye and she shot off the bed, pushing Moira out of the way (who nearly went over, still not having found her centre of gravity on the heels). 'I'd forgotten all about you,' she cooed to the A-line apparition. 'I always felt a million dollars in this.' She held the fabric next to her. 'What do you think?'

Still spiralling her arms out, Moira announced it to be 'Perfect.'

Aisling flung her robe off, and Moira wisely did not comment on the sucky-in-everything underwear her sister squeezed into as she slipped the dress over her head. It floated down around Aisling's legs, and her black mood dissolved like magic.

'If we don't leave now, we'll get stuck in the match day traffic,' Quinn bellowed outside the door.

Aisling picked up her bag, linked her arm through her sister's and strutted forth. The clothes strewn everywhere would have to wait. Hopefully Quinn had sorted Aoife and Connor: dressed them in their party best as instructed and had taken her advice to stick with the white shirt for himself. It brought out the blue in his eyes and the uncanny Ronan Keating resemblance, ensuring exceptional service from waitresses. Donal, Mammy's intended, might be the spit of Kenny Rogers but Ronan was Ireland's flavour of the month. And nobody could say life wasn't a rollercoaster now they had the twins! Aisling laughed at her little pun but quickly sobered because, soon, all would be revealed, hopefully over a lovely juicy steak.

Would Mammy become a McCarthy?

Chapter 2

♥

No. Mammy wouldn't become a McCarthy or an O'Mara-McCarthy, but the steak Aisling had ordered was cooked to medium perfection. Unfortunately, the morsel she'd been savouring had just turned to sawdust in her mouth, and she set her knife and fork down. Mammy's announcement was the last thing she would have ever expected.

She was abandoning them. Her sisters were in equal shock, although Aisling had her wits about her enough to wish Moira would close her gob. She was giving her sister a grand view of her masticated pasta. Meanwhile, Roisin was blinking manically like she always did when taken by surprise.

It wasn't fair, Aisling thought. She had been thoroughly enjoying this unexpected treat and the ambience of Beaufield Mews in spring. Their party was seated outside in the glorious sunshine amongst the cottage garden flowers with the odd lazy bee sauntering past. Mercifully, depending on whether you were a Daniel fan, the only frolicking going on in the garden was that of the children.

It was great altogether when older children, like those belonging to Donal's daughter Louise, took charge of the little ones. They'd barely seen Noah and Kiera apart from when they'd sat down long enough to shovel in the hot chips, ignoring the salad Rosi insisted upon. Anna, Donal's younger and childless daughter, was enamoured with the twins and doing a grand job keeping them entertained. As for the rest of the adults, they'd been happily ignoring the elephant in the garden of why they'd been brought together in the first place, waiting for Mammy and Donal to bring it up. The mood at the table had been convivial yet mellowed by the middle-of-the-day wine with superb food they'd been enjoying. Then Mammy spoiled it all by tapping her glass with a knife to get their attention before standing up and dropping her bombshell.

Mammy and Donal were going away for three months, THREE MONTHS, on a cruise ship that did a regular Los Angeles to Cabo San-something seven nights return sailing with a stop at somewhere Mexican sounding, beginning with M, and Puerto Vallarta along the way. However, they weren't going as mere long-time passengers with a Mexican Riviera obsession. Oh no: they were to be the entertainment. Equally as shocking, they were leaving in one week to spend a couple of days in Los Angeles with Patrick, Cindy and the babby Brianna before boarding the boat.

'But how?' Louise, who was nowhere near as shell-shocked given she had Anna to rely upon for babysitting services, asked. Meanwhile Anna, whose life would continue as usual, was unperturbed. 'Sounds like fun. Good for you!' she said before making silly faces at a giggling Aoife and Connor. As for the O'Mara girl's menfolk, they'd picked up on their partners' unhappiness at the bombshell Maureen had dropped and were all whistling and looking up at the sky.

'Well, to cut a long story short,' Maureen began, and all three of her daughters simultaneously groaned and rolled their eyes. This statement was an anomaly because this woman could turn going to the corner shop to fetch milk into a soap opera.

'Make yourselves comfortable, lads, Anna and Louise,' Roisin muttered, receiving a glare from Mammy.

CHAPTER 2   11

'That's the sort of remark I'd expect from Moira, not you, Rosi. We'll put it down to your hormones being all over the show, shall we?'

Roisin said nothing, settling back in her seat with her hands resting on the beachball curve of her belly. Shay patted her shoulder. Then, they all listened to the convoluted tale involving The Gamblers, a Kenny Rogers tribute band. Donal was the frontman of the band of four while Maureen was the tambourinist and guest singer. It had transpired that John, the drummer, knew a fella, and this fella knew another fella who was friendly with an Irish fella in a country music band that did the cruise ship rounds; they'd had to break a contract performing on the *Mayan Princess* due to a fed-up wife, a broken foot, and RSI of the wrist, respectively. This Irish fella instantly thought of The Gamblers and, aware they were all enjoying their golden retirement years, wondered if the band could fill the gap at the last minute.

It would seem they could and would because Maureen finished her story with, 'The lads were eager for sunshine, sea and adventure and there are no Gamblers without Donal. And, you know yourselves, it's always been on my bucket list to perform on a cruise ship, so it was a yes from all of us.' Maureen paused to sip her wine.

Was it? Aisling glanced at her sisters and knew they were thinking what she was thinking. One of these days, they would ask for written evidence of this never-ending bucket list of Mammy's.

Donal, beaming, added, 'Our accommodation on the ship is included in the contract. We get discounted meals, although the alcohol's not included in that. In return, we're expected to mix and mingle with guests and perform a regular evening set, and we've to host the Haybale Hoedown Evening which involves a line dancing competition on the second to last night of the cruise. We've been rehearsing your classic line dancing hits around the clock.'

This fell on deaf ears where the O'Mara girls were concerned. They were stuck on the news Mammy and Donal would be away for three months.

'But Mammy, I don't understand why you have to go. Aside from it being on your bucket list. I mean, it's only the two songs you sing, after all.' Moira flicked her silky black hair back over her shoulder.

'She has a point, Mammy. Nobody will miss the Dolly and Sheena songs,' Roisin said.

Aisling looked at both her sisters and decided there was nothing further she could add other than, 'And what about your grandchildren who love their Nana and Poppa D? They won't even know you after three months.' This wasn't true of Noah and Kiera but was for the twins.

'And I'll be fit to burst. What if I go into early labour?' Roisin piped up again.

'Aside from three months being far too long for Donal and myself to spend apart, neither of us is prepared to let the rest of the band down and I'll have you know "We've Got Tonight" and "Islands in the Stream" bring the house down every time we belt them out, don't they, Donal?'

'They do, Mo.'

'And you're forgetting I also play the tambourine, Moira.'

'I hadn't actually, Mammy,' Aisling – forever the brown-noser – butted in, ruining her favourite daughter status by adding, 'But it's hardly a vital instrument.'

'It helps keep the rhythm, thanks very much.' Maureen's eyes narrowed in her middle daughter's direction. 'And your Stevie Nicks wan would tell you to wash your mouth out, Aisling O'Mara.'

'O'Mara-Moran, Mammy.'

Aisling felt a foot nudge her and, glancing around the table, saw Moira mouthing, 'Ladies' loo, now.' She must have already told Roisin because she was getting up from the table and saying the baby was sitting on her bladder.

'And mine's been destroyed since the twins,' Aisling muttered, hot on her sister's heels.

Moira hurried after them, shouting back to the adults watching them scarper bemusedly the first thing that came to mind. 'IBS!'

Maureen called after them, 'But I didn't tell you the best bit.'

None of them stopped.

Chapter 3

'Mammy didn't follow us, did she?' Roisin asked, eyeing the door to the Ladies' as it closed behind Moira a good minute later.

'No,' Moira sounded breathless.

'What took you so long?' Aisling asked. 'Were you after doing a few circuits of the gardens before joining us?'

'No. It's the heels. They were like tent pegs, being driven into the ground with each step. I'm sure I heard Noah say I looked like a Flamingo.'

'He's very astute, our nephew. If your dress was pink, you'd be the spit of one with your storky legs,' Aisling said.

'Flamingo, not stork,' Moira rebutted.

'He's going through an ornithology phase,' Roisin said.

'What's teeth got to do with birds?' This from Moira.

'That's orthodontistry, you eejit.' Aisling shook her head.

'That coming from the eejit with a green tooth.'

Scuttling over to the mirror, Aisling grinned and winced at the parsley stuck between her incisor and the other tooth.

Roisin clapped her hands. 'You two cut it out, or we'll miss dessert at this rate.'

That silenced Aisling at least while Moira huffed over what had seen them gather in the toilets in the first place. 'Honestly, can you believe how selfish they're being? I mean, swanning

CHAPTER 3

back and forth along the Mexican Riviera while we're left here toiling away in old Dublin town.'

'I know. What about Mammy and Donal's responsibilities?' Aisling was trying to use a strand of hair as dental floss. 'And you could have told me about the green tooth, Rosi.'

'I was about to when Mammy tapped her wine glass,' Roisin said, then forgetting Aisling's tooth. 'I rely on her to look after Noah after school when I'm taking the yoga classes.'

'So do I, and Donal too. You know they have Kiera one day a week. I mean, it's just not right. You can't be hands-on grandparents like so and then just up and leave. It's, it's . . .' Moira was trying to find the right word.

'Selfish is what it is,' Aisling repeated Moira's earlier sentiment, triumphantly dislodging the green leaf. 'She better not expect us to look after Pooh while they're away.' Mammy and Donal's poodle was high maintenance.

The trio stewed in silence until Moira accidentally set the hand dryer off.

'Whoops.'

'You don't think we're the ones being selfish, do you?' Roisin ventured.

Aisling and Moira glanced at one another. Roisin had always been the weakest link.

'Technically speaking, Noah, Kiera, Aoife and Connor are our children. Our responsibility,' Roisin added.

'It takes a village to raise a child,' Aisling stated piously. She relied on Mammy and Donal too, even though Mammy could be very annoying and Donal was her 'yes' man. They were only a phone call away, which was comforting because having twins wasn't easy. At sea, they'd be uncontactable until the ship was in port. She quelled the rising panic at the thought of not being able to ring whenever the urge took her by reminding herself she did have her sisters and Quinn, of course. Hadn't Mammy raised four children of her own, Donal two? Maybe it was their time to shine. Aisling said this out loud.

Moira's eyes narrowed. 'You've had too much wine in the sun.'

'Think about it, Moira,' Aisling said, and Roisin eyeballed her until she gave her a slight shrug.

'I suppose I could get Mammy and Donal to make a recording of the "Islands in the Stream" song for when Kiera needs it, and Tom's mammy loves taking her to nursery.'

'You could.' Aisling nodded, and Roisin murmured in agreement.

'Shall we go and tell them they've our blessing to go then?'

'Erm Moira, they don't actually need our blessing. It might be better if we just show some enthusiasm.' Roisin opened the door to the restaurant. 'Come on, before they send out a search party.'

The conversation when they returned to the table was animated and jovial, as though it was perfectly normal for all three O'Mara sisters to shoot off to the toilets like they'd rockets under their arses. Maureen looked from one to the other of her girls as they sat down, and her shoulders stiffened slightly. Her suspicious expression said she didn't believe for a moment they'd synchronised bladders.

Roisin assumed the role of spokesperson as the oldest of the three. She rubbed her hands together a little too enthusiastically. 'It's very exciting. This gigging on a cruise, Mammy and Donal.'

Moira and Aisling were nodding along in an excited or eejitty manner, whichever way you interpreted it.

'Thank you, girls, but I didn't get to tell you the rest of the news.'

What now? Aisling thought, steeling herself because Mammy looked fit to burst.

'We get a family cruise discount!'

The O'Mara sisters exchanged a quick glance hearing this, wondering where it was leading. Moira opened her mouth, but Mammy silenced her.

CHAPTER 3   17

'Donal, would you like to tell them?'

Donal was beaming. 'Certainly, Mo. We've already told everyone else, but you know I came into an unexpected windfall when my Aunt Agnes passed. She'd no children of her own and left all her worldly goods to myself and my siblings.'

Aisling didn't recall hearing about this Aunt Agnes. Moira and Roisin had blank expressions, too.

'So, I told Mo that three months is a long time away from the family. You know yourself we'll miss the grandchildren terribly. Why don't we use the money from Aunt Agnes to treat you all? Of course, Mo thought this was a grand idea and, as such, we'd like you to join us on the *Mayan Princess* in a month once we've got the lay of the ship for a week's cruise down the Mexican Riviera. Patrick, Cindy, and the babby Brianna will be joining us. It's an excellent opportunity to get all the family together,' he smiled fondly at his daughters.

Aisling did the rapid blinking thing Roisin was prone to when taken unawares. Still, after hearing her sisters' excited exclamations, she swiftly recovered and joined in thanking Donal and Mammy for their generosity. The conversation around the table grew animated once more as they all talked over one another about what to pack, whether they'd see those virile, oiled-up cliff divers like on the *Love Boat*, and who was prone to getting seasick.

Aisling was privately thinking about the buffet. She'd heard wonderful things.

Roisin was wondering whether yoga sessions were available on the ship. If not, she'd offer to run a few classes.

Moira was clenching everything and hoping against hope there was a toddler club because Noah had just appeared at the table to make an announcement of his own.

Kiera had just tried to eat a worm.

When this didn't have the shock value reaction he'd hoped for, he planted his hands on his hips and sized up the adults around the table. 'Why's everybody all excited?'

Gosh, his face was so like his mam's, Aisling thought. This was a good thing, given his father was a chinless feck.

Roisin spoke up. 'Nana and Poppa D have arranged for us to have a wonderful holiday on a big cruise ship, Noah.'

'Can Mr Nibbles and Stef come? Oh, and Pooh?' Noah referenced his notoriously naughty pet gerbils and his nana and Poppa D's poodle, with whom he got on well.

'No!' was unanimously chimed.

'Mammy, and this goes for you too, Donal,' Aisling said. 'Don't be reenacting the scene from the *Titanic* on the prow of the ship while you're onboard, do you hear me?'

'Oh, don't be worrying about that, Aisling. Sure, you were there. I ticked that off my bucket list when you and I were on the ferry to Wales.'

As if I'd ever forget, Aisling thought.

Chapter 4

♥

It was a bustling Saturday afternoon in the seaside village of Howth. Maureen clutched a paper bag containing a cream slice for Ciara with a 'C'. She thought she received better service from the young shop assistant by sweetening her up whenever she called into the boutique for fashion advice. So far, Ciara hadn't put her wrong, apart from her and Bronagh's unfortunate double act at the babby Brianna's christening. Still, she wasn't one for holding a grudge and, in Maureen's opinion, everybody deserved a second chance. Since stumbling across the shop's treasure trove of clothes a few years back and discovering how flattering a wrap dress could be on a woman of certain years (thanks to Ciara), she'd felt a million dollars on the fashion front.

Today, she was flanked by Roisin, Aisling and Moira, who'd been eager to come along and help her buy the remaining items on her cruise ship wardrobe list. They were busily scoffing the cream slices they'd wheedled out of her by claiming favouritism where Ciara was concerned. Maureen had given in to their demands when the Piratey-looking man in the bakery, with the bandana and hoop earring, clacked his tongs menacingly at her due to the lengthening queue.

This afternoon's outing was thanks to Donal, who'd thoughtfully offered to mind the grandchildren while the girls helped her shop until she dropped. They were each hoping to find something suitable for the *Mayan Princess*'s formal night, too. Quinn and Tom were in intensive training for the next Dublin marathon, insisting their training programme wasn't flexible enough to include prams and a bolshy toddler. As for Shay, his music festival work had taken him away to the wilds of Scotland.

He was a good man, was her Donal, Maureen thought, pushing her sunglasses up the bridge of her nose and smiling over the scene they'd left behind. Donal had been crawling about the living room floor on all fours, giving Noah a horsey-back ride while Kiera chanted, 'Gee-up, Nob-nob!' Maureen had tried to tell her it should be 'Gee-up, Poppa D!' given he was the horse but the little girl had pouted at her nana, momentarily transporting Maureen back in time because she was the image of Moira as a tot. Then, with her eyes gleefully glinting, Kiera turned the volume up on the 'Nobbing'. There were no flies on that one and the more they'd tried to get her to say 'Noah' instead, the more she'd insisted on 'Nob'. As for the twins, bless them, they'd been happily chewing on rusks while watching the living room race-day shenanigans. She'd be sure to pick Donal up a cream slice on the way home. Maureen frowned: then again, perhaps not. It would be enough of a challenge keeping Donal away from all the creamy desserts she'd heard were on offer aboard the cruise ships as it was!

Maureen had chosen to wear a cotton shift dress for easy whipping on and off in the fitting room, and it swished around her legs as she marched past the pub. People were spilling from its open door onto the pavement, clutching pints and basking in the April sunshine. It was always the same when the sun shone. The locals were fond of pretending they were in the South of France when the mercury rose above twenty. Still and all, she thought it was a glorious day to be alive, breathing in the briny air and soaking up the jovial atmosphere the good weather had brought.

Sure, she was blessed, Maureen thought. She adored her life here in Howth, and not only did she have an ever-expanding family who loved her, but she also had the love of a good man. They shared a grand house herself and Donal, up on the hill with a sea view no less, which Maureen knew was the envy of all her friends. She belonged to so many community groups she'd lost count and, in between times, lavished attention upon her beloved grandchildren. Those dark days after her beloved Brian's death seemed a long time ago now. Since she'd met Donal the sun always seemed to shine down upon her, even when it was raining. Her cup runneth over!

'Mammy, look where you're going!' Moira yanked her back.

Too busy waxing lyrical about life, she'd been about to step straight into the path of a lycra-clad cyclist who was whizzing up the lane. *Cup runneth over*, she thought. *More like cyclist runneth over!* 'Thanks a million, Moira. I was miles away. And don't be talking with your mouthful. It wasn't a heathen I raised.' Maureen returned to her musings, thinking how well it had all worked out given the short notice this cruise had involved. Her friends and family had stepped up to the mark, coming on board with the idea.

Rosemary Farrell and her manfriend Cathal, who was in the shoe business, had said they'd be delighted to look after Pooh while she and Donal were away. Pooh was fond of Rosemary and Cathal and had stayed with them before, so she didn't need to worry about him. It was a great weight off her mind, and she'd already drawn up a list of the poodle's likes and dislikes for Rosemary to attach to the fridge. It had filled two pages. The country music compilation CD that helped soothe him when he was anxious was sitting on the table, ready to drop off tomorrow, along with all the rest of the paraphernalia that came with a poodle. Honestly, she'd more to cart around for Pooh than Aisling did the twins!

Rosemary had been pea green when she'd heard about Maureen and Donal's upcoming adventure, especially when Maureen told her that, yes, line dancing was a feature on the *Mayan Princess*'s 'at sea' days and that she would be a judge in the Haybale and Hoedown party's line dancing competition. She wouldn't be surprised if Rosemary wasn't ringing around at this very moment to see whether she could muscle in on the act and get a cruise ship gig giving talks on rambling after hip replacements. As for Cathal, though, what would he do? Maureen thought hard momentarily because she didn't think there was much call for cobblers on cruises.

Oh, what an adventure she and Donal would have cruising up and down the Mexican Riviera, no less! How exotic it sounded. She sighed happily, thinking of the endless blue sea, sky and glorious sunsets while sipping on a Pina Colada. It was hard to imagine not thinking about what was for breakfast, lunch or dinner for three months! And best of all, she'd have her whole family, including Donal's, around her for a week to enjoy it all, too. To think that in under forty-eight hours, she'd be cuddling the babby Brianna over there in Los Angeles and checking in on Patrick!

Maureen felt like jumping in the air and clicking her heels together, just like Fred Astaire in those classic old films. Her mind turned to her forebearers, who'd had to spend weeks below deck on big ships to go abroad, and she thought about what a wonderful thing international air travel was. Then, remembering she would be spending months below decks abroad, she realised she'd reached the boutique and was grateful for the distraction of the mannequin posed in the window.

Moira, Aisling and Roisin, who'd been far too busy scoffing their cream slices to bother making conversation, came to a halt, too. All four O'Mara women stared in the window at the mannequin with the red wig and hip thrust forth like she was doing one of Roisin's bendy yoga moves. She was draped in

CHAPTER 4   23

a floaty, floral handkerchief number with sparkles around the bustline.

'I like those rhinestones.' Maureen blinked, mesmerised by the sparkles.

'Sure, you're a magpie when it comes to anything shiny, Mammy,' Roisin said. 'Personally, I'd like it better with a paisley pattern. Not that it would fit me at the moment.' She laughed and clasped her hands around her tummy. 'It's a paisley tent I'll be needing.'

'I'd wear it if it was shorter,' Moira mused. 'Like, way shorter.'

'Is it cut on the bias?' Aisling asked. 'Because if it is, I can't wear it. Bias cuts make my thighs look twice their size. I can't be doing with a bias cut.'

Nobody knew the answer, so Maureen clapped her hands, 'Come on, girls, we can't stand outside gawping all afternoon. Ciara's a fount of fashion knowledge. She's bound to know the answer.'

Hearing the door jangle, Ciara looked up from the magazine she'd been flicking through with a guilty expression, quickly closing it and hiding it under the counter. Then, presumably because it was Maureen and her entourage and not her boss wondering why the boxes beside the counter remained unpacked, she relaxed. The fawning and fussing between her and Maureen saw Moira pull a gagging face at her sisters.

'Ciara, tell me now, is that dress in the window cut on the bias?'

'It is, Maureen, yes.'

'Well, that's me out,' Aisling said, huffing off to flick through the racks.

'Myself and the girls are going cruising, only I'm going for three months as crew. They've come to help me pick out the remaining essentials on my cruise wardrobe list under your expert eye.'

'How exciting. I didn't know you were a sailor, Maureen,' Ciara gushed, scooping cream from the edges of her slice and popping her finger in her mouth.

'Fecky brown-noser,' Moira whispered to her sisters, making them grin.

'As it happens, Ciara, I am a member of the Howth Yacht Club, and I have had sailing lessons, but a cruise ship is out of the realm of my experience.'

'I'd say so, considering you can't even parallel park, Mammy,' Aisling said, 'Can you imagine her trying to steer a cruise ship into port?'

Moira and Roisin sniggered.

'I'm sailing onboard the *Mayan Princess* as tambourinist and cameo singer with The Gamblers, Ciara – you know, Donal's tribute band? It won't all be play and no work, though.'

'Other way around, Mammy.'

Maureen ignored Aisling. 'We've duties to fill, Ciara, including a Haybale and Hoedown night and line dancing competition. The girls, my son and their families, along with Donal's side of the family, will be joining us for a week's holiday next month once we've had a chance to settle into the swing of ship life. So, the girls here will need something to wear for the ship's formal night. Oh, it's going to be wonderful.' Then, side-eying her offspring added, 'Although if they carry on with the smart arse remarks, they might find it's not too late to revoke their invitations.'

'If she fecking well invites Ciara with a 'C' on the cruise, I'll toss her overboard,' Moira muttered.

'Now then, Ciara, as you know, you're my one-stop shop. Well, aside from knickers, of course. I dashed into Marks yesterday.' She shuddered. 'The traffic was a nightmare but everybody knows you can't go on your holidays without new knickers and nobody does a comfortable brief for the hot weather like Marks and Spencer. Underwear needs to be able to breathe.'

'Mammy!' All three girls chimed.

Still pulling a face, Moira said, 'Don't be talking about knickers breathing or saying things like "One Stop Shop", Mammy, it's very annoying.' She was distracted by a green micro mini dress, which she pulled out for inspection.

'Don't you be saying things like that to me either, or you'll find yourself at home in an Irish summer while the rest of us are basking there on the Mexican Riviera. And you can put that back where you found it, Moira O'Mara. Think on. They've a strict dress code on the cruise ships, so they do. There's no showing your arse to your fellow passengers allowed.'

Moira looked sceptical but did as she was told.

'But I thought you were working as crew, like?' Ciara, non-plussed, studied her finger, which was full of cream.

'I am. It's a working holiday. I'm confident I'll find everything on that list right here.' She smoothed the paper she'd fetched from her bag under the younger woman's nose.

'And Ciara, what have you got that's not cut on the bias?' Aisling piped up.

'This is pretty,' Roisin was saying to no one in particular, having found a halter neck dress with plenty of room around the middle.

'You'd want to be careful on the open decks wearing that, Rosi.' Maureen was frowning. 'I'd imagine it can get very blowy out on the open sea, and that yoke there would spend more time up round your ears than floating about your knees.'

'That's a good point you're after making there, Mammy.' Roisin hung the dress back on the rack.

'Fecky brown-noser,' Moira said out the corner of her mouth to her big sister before holding out a black cocktail dress just above the knees. 'What about this then?'

'Definitely warmer, Moira, but I think we've still room for—' Whatever Maureen had been about to say fell away as, like a moth to the flame, she zeroed in on a shimmering swathe of fabric. It was a rose between thorns.

'Ah, no, stand back,' Moira muttered, flattening herself against the rack. 'She's got that look.'

'It's that gleam in her eyes. The one she gets whenever she thinks she's spotted Daniel Day-Lewis in the wild,' Aisling said and, having no wish to be trampled, she scuttled over to the safety of the fitting room, dragging Roisin and her unborn child with her.

Maureen stamped over to the object of her desire. She snatched out a silver lamé, full-length gown, hungrily seeking the label, then held the dress to her chest, announcing with the same fervour usually reserved for her Hail Marys: 'It's in my size! I knew I could count on you, Ciara.'

Ciara puffed up, pleased with herself, while Aisling whispered to Roisin, 'She hasn't done anything except eat her cream slice.'

Maureen made a beeline for the fitting room, and Aisling and Roisin stepped aside as though they were bouncers outside a nightclub.

'It's perfect,' Maureen said, hanging it up. 'Sure, it's just what Dolly would wear.'

'Dolly has a teeny-tiny waist, though, Mammy.'

'Moira O'Mara, read my lips. You're skating on thin ice, my girl.' Maureen wrenched the curtain closed.

Chapter 5

♥

'What an afternoon!' Maureen declared, closing the front door and returning to the living room. 'They've finally gone.'

Donal was picking up the last of the toys strewn across the living room floor with one hand resting in the crook of his back. Pooh watched him from his bed, guarding the colourful stacking rings he'd commandeered off the twins earlier.

'It was very good of you to look after all four children, Donal. Thanks to you, I'm all kitted out now for the cruise, and the girls are happy with the dresses and trouser suit they found for when they join us. Who'd have thought Aisling would look so well in a trouser suit but she does.' Then, veering into the kitchen added, 'I could murder a cup of tea. You?'

'Are you sure they've gone, Mo?' Donal's eyes darted nervously about the open space to where she stood with a kettle in hand. 'You know what they're like. They have a habit of returning, not that I don't love them all dearly. It's just I'm knackered, so I am.'

'I'm sure.' Maureen laughed, filling the kettle and, over the noise of the tap, said, 'It took forever for Moira and Aisling to load the children and all their paraphernalia into the car.' Roisin and Noah, who'd walked the short distance home, would have reached their front door in the time it took for

Moira's old banger to splutter off down the drive. She turned the tap off with a shake of her head. 'Life was simpler when we were young parents, Donal. You'll remember. It was a case of chucking them in the backseat and boot.' Maureen mimed a forward pass, 'And off you went.'

'You're not wrong there, Mo. And I'm feeling far from young at the moment. These knees and back of mine are well past their best before date.'

'That's what you get for giddying Noah about the living room on your hands and knees.' Maureen tutted.

Donal staggered bow-legged to his armchair, and he sank down in it. 'It wasn't Noah, Mo. He's light as a feather. I barely noticed he was on my back.'

'You weren't after playing the Twister game again, were you? That thing should come with a warning: "Not suitable for anyone over the age of forty".'

Donal gave her a wry grin. 'No. It was Kiera, as it happens, but I've only myself to blame because if you do the horsey-back rides for one you've got to do it for the other, and she made it clear she wasn't missing out.'

'She's a strong will on her that wan, just like her mammy, and she's the build of her Aunty Aisling at that age. I had to bend my knees to plop her in the bath back in the day.' Maureen set about making the tea, listening as Donal told her how, struggling to clamber aboard Poppa D's back, Noah had suggested his cousin use the chair in which he was now sitting as a mounting block.

'Only she didn't just climb on my back: she leapt. Dear God, Mo, it was like an enormous sack of potatoes landing on me, so it was.'

Maureen was laughing despite herself. 'Sack of potatoes? That's our granddaughter you're talking about!' She carried the tea over and then sat down herself. 'Where's the remote, Donal? Our show's about to start.'

CHAPTER 5   29

Donal patted about the chair, lifting his backside and locating it there. He took aim at the television and the screen filled with the grinning face of the game show host. Maureen settled back in her chair, sipping her tea and trying to guess the answers before the contestants. Meanwhile, Donal only made it halfway through his brew before his head lolled back, and he began snoring.

As the credits rolled, half an hour later, Maureen's mind turned to the bags she'd yet to unpack waiting for her on the bed. Now was as good a time as any to finish packing her suitcase.

Maureen delved into the bag and pulled out the wafting-about poolside caftan; she rolled it neatly and placed it in the open case on the bed, eyeing the rest of the packed items. It wouldn't be easy condensing three months into one suitcase, but from what she'd heard the cabins aboard the cruise ships were cosy. She'd no wish for herself and Donal to be like those children in the Narnia books Aisling had enjoyed as a child, wading through clothes to get to what lay beyond the wardrobe or, rather, cabin door. Her list was keeping her in check and proving to be a Godsend.

Next came the nautical-themed t-shirt, then the casual day dress – linen, of course, for breathability in the hot weather. It was a shame knickers didn't come in the linen, too, she mused. Mind, they might be a bit scratchy. The piece de resistance, however, was her silver lamé gown. The moment she'd slid the zipper into place and admired herself in the fitting room mirror, she'd known they were a match made in heaven. She wouldn't roll it for fear of any of the silvery lamé falling off. Instead, she'd fold it carefully and lay it over the packed items.

Of course, the girls thought all that silver was over the top but they were hardly fashion connoisseurs, despite what they liked to think. They didn't understand that being over the top was the whole point because Dolly was larger than life. Life was too short to be a wallflower.

They'd made a pit stop on their way home. Her first port of call was to revisit the nautical-themed café where she told the girls to wait outside because she'd not wish to be threatened with the tongs by your piratey man a second time. Then, clasping a bag with two more cream slices, she told them they were making a stop at Carrick's the Cobblers because she wanted a word with Rosemary Farrell. 'I've had an epiphany, girls.'

This was met with a groan.

Maureen didn't care as she hurried along because she remembered something while in that fitting room twirling in her lamé. Rosemary had recently trod the boards at the local church hall as Melanie in *Gone with the Wind* for the Howth Retired (But Not From Life) Amateur Dramatic Society's annual production. She'd auditioned for the role of Scarlett O'Hara, disappointed and a tad bitter, truth be told, to lose out to Bold Brenda who'd managed to get Scarlett's coquettish aura down pat.

Personally, Maureen thought Rosemary was a little long in the tooth to play Melanie on what she fancied had been the longest night of her life, watching the play adapted straight from the film on a hard wooden pew. The show had dragged on and on, and Donal, who could sleep with his eyes open when the need arose, had nodded off. She'd had to nudge him awake, however, when he began snoring as your wan who always ate all the sausage rolls after the bowls said the line everybody had been waiting for, 'Frankly my dear—' Nobody had heard the rest because of Donal's snore.

Rosemary had donned a platinum, Southern Belle-style wig as part of her costume. She'd confided in Maureen that she'd

CHAPTER 5   31

kept it because Cathal was partial to her as a blonde. The mind boggled as to what Cathal and Rosemary got up to after hours. In-hours, for that matter, given how many times the 'back in five minutes' sign was hung in the window.

The cream slices had worked a treat and soon they'd been puffing and panting up the hill toward home. Maureen liked to look the part and was determined to channel Dolly for her performances on the *Mayan Princess*. She'd cross the Sheena Eastern bridge when she came to it.

With Donal snoring in the living room, Maureen decided to have a quick try-on. She slipped into her silver dress and tucked her hair under the bouffant blonde wig. A swipe of glossy pink lippy and taking a step back from the dressing table mirror, her eyes widened. She was the image of Dolly, albeit not as well-endowed. Still, this called for a song, and she broke into 'Jolene' even though it wasn't on The Gambler's playlist. Her voice urged Jolene not to take her man when the phone rang. She'd best answer it because by the time Donal roused himself from his chair whoever it was would have rung off.

Indeed, a moment later, as she shuffled forth, Donal was still half-asleep; he'd half-pulled himself out of his chair but catching sight of a silver lamé-wearing, blonde wigged vision, he fell back into it clutching his chest.

'Donal, it's me, Maureen.'

'Mo?'

'Mo,' Maureen confirmed, reaching for the phone.

'For a moment, I thought you were RuPaul!'

There was no time to dwell on this as Maureen answered the call with an inexplicable Tennessee accent, still in Dolly mode. Her eyes narrowed, realising it was one of those annoying bang-on-tea-time telemarketers, and she curtly replied, 'No, we do not need a Tenerife timeshare opportunity. We're heading away on a cruise ship for three months in a few days.' Then, putting the phone down on the bench with a clunk, glared over at Donal.

He pushed his glasses on. 'Ah, now I can see it, Mo. You're Dolly's double, so you are.'

Mollified, Maureen was about to give him a 'Jolene' rendition when she saw two faces appear at the French doors. Terence and Amanda, their neighbours. Their mouths were agape, clocking Maureen.

Donal let them in while Pooh yipped and yapped.

'Sorry if we're interrupting a spot of role-playing,' Terence said over the ruckus. 'I always said they were a pair of sly dogs, these two, didn't I, Amanda?'

Amanda nodded. 'You did, Terence.'

'There is nothing at all untoward going on,' Maureen informed the neighbours she knew were part of the Howth swinging scene. 'I'm trying on my Dolly costume for the cruise.'

'Dolly?' Terence frowned, bewildered. 'I thought you were RuPaul.'

'So did I,' Amanda agreed.

Maureen pulled the wig off in a huff, tossing it aside, deciding she wouldn't be asking these two to join herself and Donal in the garden to enjoy a pre-dinner aperitif.

'We did knock at the front but nobody answered,' Amanda explained, batting her lashes at Donal. 'We were off for our evening stroll and remembered your list, Maureen. Do you have it ready?'

Donal moved behind Pooh.

'The list. Right-ho.' Maureen tore a page off the pad by the phone headed, 'Amanda and Terence's To Do List'. Their neighbours had kindly offered to water the garden in the unlikely event of an Irish heatwave while they were away, bring the bins in and keep a general eye on the house. It wasn't a long list but Maureen liked to get things in writing. She folded it in half, aware of Terence giving her another slow once over as she passed it to his wife. 'Roisin will have the front door key and her phone number's on the list if there are any problems.

CHAPTER 5

And this is a small thank you for your troubles.' She fetched the box of Celebrations.

'You needn't have, but thank you.' Amanda's tone suggested they were posher, Thornton's-chocolates sort of people.

Maureen and Donal saw them off and, deciding she should get out of her silver gown before she managed to spill something on it, Maureen disappeared to the bedroom again to change and finish packing.

She'd just laid the dress down on top of all the other items in her case and was about to close it when Donal shouted for help. Maureen, picking up on the note of panic in his voice, wondered what was going on as she wasted no time bursting through to the living room, half-expecting to see him bailed up by Amanda.

The sight she was met with brought her up short as it burned into her retinas, making her momentarily freeze. Then, leaping into action, she yelled, 'Pooh, get off that!'

The poodle, in seventh heaven, ignored her.

'Mo, I think he thinks your wig there is a female bichon frisé the way he's going at it.'

'Donal, do something!'

'I've been trying but, each time I get near it, he nips at me.'

'What exactly does he hope to achieve? I mean, he's been seen to.'

'I would think that's fairly obvious, Maureen.'

Chapter 6

♥

The Cruise - Day 1

The ship might be the biggest cruise liner Maureen had ever seen. However, the cabin they would call home for the next three months aboard the majestic *Mayan Princess* was minuscule. With Donal peering over her shoulder in the doorway, Maureen told him they would frame their living quarters in a positive light. 'Think cosy, Donal, and if we start getting claustrophobic, we can do the bendy yoga breathing.'

'Cosy, Mo,' Donal affirmed.

Now she was hanging up the last of her clothes, having just told the lads from The Gamblers to do the same when they'd swung by to see if her and Donal's couples cabin was any roomier than theirs because they were four to a cabin, bunking in with a comedian from Canada called Kevin. It wasn't. The silver lamé shimmering on its hanger caught her eye and, for a moment, she mourned the loss of the wig. It hadn't survived to make the journey with them because, by the time Pooh had finally been lured off with a doggy treat, the wig resembled a headless, self-shedding sheep. Maureen had picked up the pitiful remains and cried, 'Look at it! I'll not be wearing that now. And what will Rosemary say when she finds out Pooh had his way with her wig?'

'What Rosemary doesn't know won't hurt her. Besides, we don't want it colouring her thoughts on Pooh, given she'll be his primary caregiver while we're away. You can buy her a new one when we return, Mo.'

He was a wise man, Donal. She'd have to put 'buy a new wig' on her to do list for when they got home but, for now, it could wait. Three months was a long way away. She could hug herself at the thought of twelve whole weeks of not thinking about meal planning! A teeny-tiny cabin was a small price to pay for that.

They were a team, Donal and herself, who worked together like a well-oiled machine, she thought, finishing her unpacking and sliding her case alongside his in the wardrobe. Sure, look at how they'd seamlessly implemented an effective unpacking system to combat the space-challenged cabin whereby Donal had hung his things up in the closet first while she'd filled her half of the drawers; then, they'd swapped. She could not think of anyone else she'd like to share a teeny-tiny cabin with.

Maureen pondered what to wear for the Sail Away party, which they would soon head to the Lido deck for. As she eyed the tummy-control swimsuit and carefully picked poolside caftan brought at her Howth boutique a few days ago, she murmured, 'Sail Away party.'

'Did you say something, Mo?'

'I was just thinking that life will be ticking over in its usual fashion at home while we're about to sip cocktails at a Saily Away party.

Donal chortled from where he was perched on the bed's edge, flicking through television channels. 'I know what I'd rather be doing.'

Maureen half-wished she hadn't told Patrick and Cindy not to hang about when they'd dropped them at the Port of Los Angeles as the babby Brianna was due a nap. It would have been nice to have family there to wave them off like they were embarking on an epic voyage. Still, Pat liked to get his head down whenever Brianna did so it was best they drove home to their apartment. She'd be sure he got plenty of rest and relaxation on his holiday aboard the ship. Smiling to herself, she thought, *Once a mother, always a mother*. No matter how old your children are! What a joy it had been spending time with her youngest grandchild these last few days and witnessing all her new tricks first-hand. They'd arranged with Pat and Cindy to meet for lunch when the ship was back in port next week for a few hours between it sailing off again. Her youngest grandchild, Brianna Buttercup O'Mara, was an absolute dote even if the poor love had Buttercup as a middle name.

So much had had to be done to make this stint aboard the *Mayan Princess* happen that it made her head spin. There'd been lunch with the family to tell them their plans and invite them on holiday, the shopping trip with her girls, packing, passing out lists of instructions and entrusting Rosemary and Cathal with Pooh's care. And she wouldn't allow herself to think about the tearful airport scene that had carried on for so long that the airline had paged her and Donal.

'Are you ready, Mo?' Donal asked, setting the remote down.

'Nearly.' Maureen's voice was drowned out by a groaning from the ship's bowels below their cabin. 'That'll be the engine warming up.' She said, swiftly wriggling into her swimsuit, pulling on a pair of floaty trousers, and slipping the caftan over the top. Then, ducking into the bathroom and banging her elbow on the wall, she rubbed it, eying the shower and wondering how Donal – who would be like Gulliver in this bathroom that could well have been built for Lilliputians – would get on.

'Mo!'

She wished she had a flower to tuck behind her ear as she quickly swiped on some lippy and fluffed her hair.

CHAPTER 6   37

'What do you think?' She popped out of the bathroom and, if there'd been room, she'd have given Donal a twirl.

'You're every inch a Mayan princess, Mo.'

Maureen smiled, noting Donal was getting a second airing from the shirt she'd bought him for the Hawaiian-themed housewarming party they'd held not long after moving into Magnolia Mews. 'Thank you,' she fluttered her lashes, 'and you look the part too.' This wasn't strictly true because a Mayan prince was likelier to have worn loin cloths than flowery luau shirts, but he'd do her!

'It's going to take us a while to become familiar with the ship's layout,' Donal said as they hung their lanyards around their necks and pushed sunglasses on their heads.

Maureen thought he wasn't wrong there a second later, turning to the left instead of the right as she exited the cabin. It was just as well Donal had a good sense of direction! She beamed at a young woman, a fellow entertainer presumably emerging from her cabin with a man appearing behind her as she padded down the narrow corridor behind Donal to the lift. *Would they all become like family?* she wondered. People often did when they were lumped together in the same boat, so to speak.

The woman was also dressed for the Sail Away party. She was wearing a bikini top and sarong and was beautiful, Maureen thought as she stood alongside them to wait for the lift. She reminded her a little of Moira only how Moira would look in another ten years. The man lagged behind, checking something on his mobile phone.

'This is mine and my manfriend Donal's first time on a cruise,' Maureen informed her. 'I'm Maureen.'

'Tomasina and that's my husband, Pawel.'

Pawel glanced up then and acknowledged them with a dip of his head.

The lift was taking forever, Maureen thought, looking up at the light to see what floor it was on.

'It's very slow, but all those stairs to the eleventh floor are daunting,' Tomasina said.

Maureen laughed and agreed they were.

'You're Irish?'

'Yes. Where are you from?'

'Poland.'

'Oh, very nice.' Maureen wouldn't have a clue whether it was or wasn't. Now she was next to the woman she decided she could pass for a Polish Demi Moore just as Moira could the Irish.

'It is. My little brother has gone to Ireland for work. He has heard there is plenty.'

'The Celtic tiger is roaring, Tomasina.' Maureen could tell by the young woman's face she might as well have been speaking a foreign language and added in plain speak, 'Yes, the country is enjoying boom times.'

This time Tomasina nodded. 'He's in Dublin.'

'Well now, would you believe that's where we're from. It's a small world, so it is. And when you do visit Dublin, you'd be very welcome to stay at O'Mara's Guesthouse. It's my family hotel, and it's in a grand location overlooking St Stephen's Green. Be sure to let Aisling, my daughter, know you were on the *Mayan Princess* with me and Donal, and she'll give you an excellent rate.'

'Thank you, Maureen. I would love that one day and for my Mama too. She is a widow and misses me and Piotr: there is only the three of us so he is the baby of our small family.'

'I'm sure she does.'

'She even misses Pawel, not that she will admit this because she blames him for taking me away but there is no work where we come from so we must travel.' She shrugged. 'I worry for Piotr. He is young, you know. He has no life experience and then just like that,' she clicked her fingers, 'he is in the big smoke on his own.'

'Don't be worrying too much, Tomasina. Dublin is a very small big city. I'm sure he'll be grand.'

Tomasina seemed reassured as she smiled at Maureen while Donal made impatient noises. Pawel put his phone away, coming to stand alongside them.

'Are you contracted as entertainers?' Maureen asked, wondering what talents this good-looking Polish couple had.

'Yes, we perform as the Dreamweaver. An illusionist act.'

'Magic, you mean?'

'I love a good magic show, me,' Donal piped up.

Tomasina and Pawel nodded. 'I was a brick layer in another life,' Pawel said. 'What about you?'

Donal opened his mouth, but Maureen got in first. 'You might have noticed that Donal here strongly resembles Kenny Rogers?'

'Who?' the husband and wife looked blank.

Maureen frowned. Perhaps Kenny wasn't big in Poland. 'Kenny Rogers is a much-loved and famous country music star in America.'

'I see.' Tomasina nodded enthusiastically, but Maureen wasn't convinced she did; nevertheless, she continued.

'Donal is the frontman for a Kenny Rogers tribute band called The Gamblers, and I duet with him on a couple of numbers and play the tambourine. It's essential for keeping the rhythm, you know.'

Again, a knowledgeable nod as a woman with light brown hair, eyes, and the sort of face that was pleasant to look at but wouldn't stick in your mind joined them to wait at the lift. Maureen put her age to be somewhere in her fifties. 'Hello there. I'm Maureen from Dublin. Well, Howth these days, to be exact, and this is my manfriend Donal.'

Maureen received a tight little smile in return and a mumbled reply, 'Carole from Sydney, Australia' before the woman's eyes slid away.

Now, it could be said and had, in fact, been said quite a lot, actually, and mainly by Maureen's daughters, that there were times she was slow on the uptake. Still, on this occasion, she took the hint that the woman wasn't in the mood to chat and, even though she was a little put out by the lack of reciprocal small talk, Maureen hadn't run O'Mara's for so many years not to have learned you never knew what was going on with a person. As such, she reserved judgment. Tomasina quizzing her about Dublin distracted her. At the same time, she waited for the lift door to finally ping open.

Maureen overheard Pawel telling Donal he and Tomasina were seasoned cruise ship entertainers. So she deftly moved the conversation away from Dublin, eager to get the low-down on what to expect from ship life over the next three months.

The lift arrived and the couple continued to fill them in on what to expect at sea. It seemed to Maureen they were in for a mixed bag of hard work, what with performing night after night, rehearsals and having to always be 'on', even off stage. Tomasina told them that as a paid performer, they were public property on the ship. If people butted in on your relaxing times to chat about your show, so be it. The living quarters were cramped, and the novelty of the buffet and cocktails wore off after a while. At this stage, Maureen found it hard to believe that not cooking and leading a cocktail lifestyle would ever get old. Tomasina was adamant, however, as was Pawel, who nodded along. Cruise ship life was an adjustment, but they were lucky to make a living doing what they loved.

Maureen was digesting this as she and Donal shuffled back to let more people in the lift. It was stopping on every floor and was soon fit to burst. 'We're full,' she mouthed, peering over the heads of her fellow passengers squished inside, in case those attempting to board on the sixth floor weren't getting the message. Then, her eyes widened as a woman astride a motorised scooter began nudging it forward with a steely look of determination. 'Quick, shut the doors!' someone said. Maureen held her breath as the door was wedged open by the scooter's front tyre but, after a moment, the woman gave up and reversed. The door slid shut, and the lift continued its laboriously slow journey.

'Did you see your woman attempting to ram raid the lift just now, Donal?' Maureen whispered.

'I did, Mo. Perhaps she was hangry and in a hurry to get to the buffet.'

'More like a pig looking into a washing machine,' Maureen muttered. 'Sure, you'd have to be dense to behave like that. Yer woman should have her licence revoked.'

Donal smiled but it had vanished by the eighth floor because of a pervasive smell.

'It's worse than Pooh when he'd had one too many doggy treats,' Maureen gasped. The stench threatened to suffocate them all. She wanted to shout, 'For the love of God, who did that?' Nobody was giving anything away, though, as they stood, hands pinned to their sides, eyes staring straight ahead. Her eyes were watering, and she saw a look of desperation come over Donal. Then, finally, the doors opened onto the eleventh floor. Maureen grasped Donal's hand and squeezed it silently, communicating her excitement and wanting to cry, 'Freedom!' He squeezed back and, losing Tomasina and Pawel in the throng, they ventured forth.

Chapter 7

♥

'Isn't it wonderful?' Maureen breathed, soaking in the scene and committing it to memory so she could email the girls the next chance she got as to what to expect. The Lido deck was alive with an infectious music beat as passengers clutching colourful cocktails milled about, avoiding being splashed by excitable children already playing in the pool. The deck chairs flanking either side of the pool were already filled as holidaymakers forgot about their worries and began unwinding. Here and there, she saw amiable crew members in crisp white uniforms chatting to passengers. The sun beat down and the air was filled with a heady mix of grilling burgers, salt, suncream and the tang of cigarette smoke.

'It is, Mo. I'll order us a couple of cocktails, shall I?'

'Grand.'

'A Pina Colada?' Donal launched into a few verses of the classic song. Still, Maureen was distracted by the vibrant blue drink a woman jiggling about to the music in barely-there shorts was clutching. 'Actually, that one there looks interesting,' Maureen interrupted him, crooning about getting caught in the rain, and hustled off to tap the blonde woman's shoulder. 'Excuse me, but what's that you're drinking?'

The woman held up the drink with its cocktail umbrella. 'It's a Blue Lagoon. Vodka, blue curacao and lemonade. It's delicious,' she twanged in an American accent before slurping it up like lolly water.

'I'll take your word for it.' Then, turning to Donal, Maureen said her favourite line from *When Harry Met Sally* film. 'I'll have what she's having.' She spied a familiar pair of bandy legs amongst the milling crowd and waved to Niall, The Gambler's guitarist. 'I'll be over there with Niall. Oh, and Donal, tell the bartender you're crew. You'll get faster service that way.' Maureen was going over to where Niall was leaning against the ship's railings when she was nearly knocked over by an overexcited child running like the wind, even though there was a sign clearly stating there was to be no running by the pool. *Children being children*, she mused with a pang for Noah.

'How're you, Niall?' Maureen reached the man, watching the Sail Away carry on with a bemused expression. She was fond of Niall. She was fond of all The Gamblers but had a soft spot for Niall, a gentle soul. He was also lonely since his wife had left him. Donal had told her she'd arrived home from her French evening class a few years ago and told him she'd met someone else who shared her passion for Provence. That was that, and he'd been on his own ever since.

'Grand, Maureen. Isn't the craic great?'

'It is, Niall. Have you seen the other lads?' She asked, referring to John the drummer, a widower with an eye for the ladies, and fat Davey, who was on the keyboard, as the lads called him. Davey was divorced and happy that way.

'John's off having a game of ping-pong, and Davey made straight for the buffet. No surprises there.'

Maureen laughed. 'I shouldn't laugh because I'm eager to check it out myself, and Donal will be pleased to hear there's ping-pong. Sure, I'll be like one of those golf widows whose husband's never home because he's swinging his club on the local green, only with the ping-pong, so I will. You know what he's like when he gets one of those bats in his hands. He morphs into the Pete Sampras of the table tennis world.'

This time Niall laughed. 'I won't be putting up my hand to play doubles with him and the lads, that's for sure. He's too competitive for my blood.'

'What's your Kevin cabin-mate like?'

'No discernible annoying habits, reasonable personal hygiene, better than Davey's. Mind, that's not saying much. He assures us he doesn't snore, unlike Davey, and for a comedian he seems a dour fella, but I imagine if you make your living making people laugh you might be all out of funnies off stage.'

'Well, Niall, he can't afford not to be cracking the jokes when he's on the ship. The passengers are king, and we, as entertainers, are expected to always entertain.' Maureen filled him in on the conversation with Tomasina and Pawel.

'So what you're saying, Maureen, is I'm to be strolling about with my guitar at all times, ready to strum a quick tune should anyone make a request? Should I stick a rose between my teeth, too, if I'm going to be doing all this serenading?'

'No, Niall.' Maureen shook her head and pointed to a woman sprawling on a sun lounger. 'Say your woman over there, with the swimsuit that is a size too small for her, clicks her fingers and asks you what your favourite Kenny song is; you can't tell her to mind your own business, you've to engage in a spot of banter with her.'

Niall looked terrified at the prospect, and Maureen decided it was time to move the conversation along so, seeing Donal on his way back with a drink that reminded her of a sunset in one hand and her Blue Lagoon in the other, she tried to convince him to step out of his comfort zone and order a cocktail instead of the ale he was supping.

'Thanks a million,' her hand shot out for the drink Donal offered as he reached them, eager for a sip. It was delicious, which she confirmed to both men. 'What's that you've got, Donal?'

CHAPTER 7   45

'This, Mo, is a Hurricane made with rum, passionfruit and lemon juice. Very nice it is, too. Although your man behind the bar was a little mean with the rum.' He held it out for her to try and they swapped drinks, agreeing they were equally scrumptious.

Maureen was swaying along to the poppy music, interrupted by a welcome-aboard message from the *Mayan Princess*'s captain. 'Doesn't Captain Franco have a masterful voice?' she gushed. 'I think we're in safe hands.'

'Actually, I thought his voice was rather high-pitched. He sounded like a Bee Gee to me,' Donal said in a most-unlike Donal manner.

Maureen detected a little of the green-eyed monster in his summation of poor Captain Franco. Still, she let it go as the ship's horn echoed across the port. She clutched Donal's arm in excitement. Her cry of, 'We're off!' was drowned out by the DJ's shout, ' Let's get this party started!' and the ensuing cheer. People thronged to join the professional dancers who'd filed into the middle of the deck area by the bar. They were decked out in their bright beachwear as they broke out the moves, waving their arms about and beckoning for passengers on the sidelines to join in. Maureen felt that surge she always got when she badly wanted to join in. It was a sort of bubbling like a volcano on the verge of erupting. A 'This is my moment to shine' sensation, which was why she'd begun jiggling everything from the neck down. She asked Donal if he fancied taking a turn on the dance floor.

'Erm, I might sit this one out, Mo.'

'Niall?'

'Ah, no, sure you're grand, Maureen. Look, there's loads up there on their own.'

'Lads, cop yourself on, we're supposed to be mixing and mingling as crew. It's in our contract.' Neither man moved as they whistled and avoided eye contact. Ah well, nobody could say she wasn't taking her role seriously as, almost breaking out into a jog and keeping a tight hold of her Blue Lagoon, she thrust her way into the thick of it all.

If the girls could see me now, she thought as an ABBA medley began to play, and she waved her free arm in the air like one of those young wans at a rave. She danced until her feet began aching, and her drink was a distant memory. Then, heading back to where Niall and Donal were relaxing, she saw they were on a second round. If you couldn't beat them, you might as well join them, she decided, veering off toward the bar.

Chapter 8

♥

Maureen and Donal had arranged to meet John, Davey and Niall outside the Lido Buffet for 7pm and, upon leaving the Sail Away party two cocktails down, decided it was a good time to explore their new home and familiarise themselves with its layout. They'd ducked into the gym, making plans to visit it thrice a week while onboard; the day spa where a hairdressing service was available; and checked out the kids' clubs for when all the grandchildren joined them. They were both delighted with how much was on offer to keep them entertained as their parents would be, too! The rest of them could help out with the little ones here and there to give Aisling, Quinn, Pat and Cindy a break.

Donal had been keen to locate the Havana Lounge, where The Gamblers would play tomorrow evening and each evening for the remainder of the week-long cruise aside from the Haybale and Hoedown evening. The country music party was to be held on the Lido deck. For now, though, they'd trooped down the stairs, inspecting the different levels, taking a few wrong turns, and pausing to check out the various table service restaurants. The menus sounded delicious but given the discount they received in the buffet restaurant that's where they'd be eating their meals. Not that either of them was complaining.

The Havana Lounge was on Level 7, and hearing the bells and whistles of a slot machine jackpot going off somewhere ahead of them, Maureen realised the casino must be on the same floor. As for the bar, it had potted palms in the corners and a bright mural depicting classic cars from the forties and fifties cruising a colourful Havana Street scene. Spanish guitar music with a strong percussion accompaniment played from hidden speakers.

'That's where we'll be playing.' Donal gestured to the space reserved on the far side of the lounge for the band and dancing.

Maureen gave the bar floor a slow sweep, concluding a few haybales about the place would give it more of a country music vibe for tomorrow night's performance, albeit a Cuban country music vibe. They'd have to locate the haybales stored away for the hoedown party and she mentioned this to Donal who agreed it would add to the ambience.

'Shall we take a peek at the Grand Theatre?' Donal suggested, studying the ship's map on the wall and, receiving the nod, headed off in the general direction of its location.

They found it without difficulty and, pushing the door open, were met with a deserted theatre in semi-darkness and a ceiling filled with thousands of twinkling stars.

'It's very grand,' Maureen whispered even though there was no one about to hear her.

Donal agreed from where he was leaning over her shoulder.

Maureen couldn't take her eyes off the empty stage. She was getting that volcano bubbling up feeling once more. 'Donal, are you thinking what I'm thinking?'

'I am, Mo. It's the biggest auditorium I will ever stand on-stage in. It's too good an opportunity not to.'

Partners in crime, they took the stairs to the stage two at a time and, a minute later, were standing in the centre of it

CHAPTER 8   49

looking up at the rows of empty seats spanning a semi-circle and stretching all the way up to a second tier of seating.

Maureen closed her eyes. 'I'm visualising a sold-out house.'

'And the entire audience is clapping and cheering for The Gamblers,' Donal added.

'It's deafening, so it is. Oh, and now, listen, can you hear the chant? It's the 'We've Got Tonight' song they're desperate to hear.'

'You're right, Mo,' Donal played along. 'We'll have to wait for them to quieten down.'

They smiled into each other's eyes, and then Donal struck a relaxed stance. At the same time, Maureen, using her fist for a microphone, never took her eyes off him, swaying gently as he began crooning the ballad. The acoustics in the theatre were terrific, even without a microphone, and Maureen couldn't wait to step in as Sheena and hear her voice reach the very last row of seats. She'd just inhaled all the way to the bottom of her lungs in readiness to join in for her part when a sinewy manchild – so skinny one eye would do him – materialised in the wings. He was wearing a tank top and tights, and Maureen kept her gaze firmly trained above his torso as he cleared his throat.

'Excuse me, but we've got a rehearsal about to take place here, and the theatre's off limits to passengers when shows or the bingo aren't on. You'll find the Karaoke in the Sundowner Bar at seven o'clock this evening.'

He'd an accent perfect for Bert, the chimney sweep in Mary Poppins, Maureen thought, indignant at the Karaoke comment. She puffed up and explained that they weren't passengers but fellow performers who'd been rehearsing themselves for the gig they were playing in the Havana Lounge tomorrow evening.

The young man placed a hand on his hip and raised an eyebrow, 'I think you'll find this isn't a designated rehearsal space for lounge bar performers.'

Maureen, not liking the affectation when he'd said 'lounge bar performers', opened her mouth to tell him that The Gamblers were held in high regard at home in Ireland and were very popular on the sixty-plus birthday circuit. Thank you very much. However, a swarm of sinewy young people in tights was flooding the stage, so she closed it again to see the young man fling his arm out yonder.

'The public exit is at the top of the stairs.'

Before Maureen could say precisely what she thought about being spoken to like so by a twelve-year-old in tights, Donal took her hand and tugged her off stage.

'Come on, Mo. I think we'd best leave them to it. Dancers can be a terrible temperamental bunch.'

'How do you know that?' Maureen asked, huffing up the stairs behind him.

'Louise did the tap for a few years as a child, and there was always someone in the class in tears over their shoes not tapping properly.'

Maureen thought about how hot under the collar some of the girls at line dancing could get when someone stepped out of sync and decided he was right. 'Look at that,' she stabbed at a poster on the wall beside the door which had just closed on the dance troupe gathering on the stage. 'Latino Stars of the Sea.' She followed this up with a harrumphing noise. 'Yer sinewy wan back there's about as Latino as I am.' She wished she had a felt tip in her bag because she'd have loved to have drawn glasses and scribbled a moustache on the pouty face striking a snake-hipped pose in the poster.

'Forget about him, Mo. He's a jumped up little so and so. Let's see what else the *Mayan Princess* has to offer.'

'You're right, Donal. I'll be the bigger person and let it go. Shall we see if we can find the photographs snapped when we came on board earlier?'

'Good idea, Mo. It might be one for the album.'

CHAPTER 8   51

They set off again and hadn't wandered far before finding themselves in a wide corridor. The portal windows allowed natural light to flood in, and they paused to admire the vista of blue while on their right expensively framed paintings lined the wall.

Thanks to the informative newsletter, Maureen knew these artworks would be auctioned off throughout the week at the scheduled Champagne Art Auctions. She looked forward to sipping champagne while contemplating an eclectic range of paintings. Maureen and Donal meant to make the most of everything on the ship this first week at sea and expected, after a few weeks, the novelty of a champagne lifestyle might wear off a little but, right now, that was hard to imagine. She focused on the paintings: encompassing everything from fine to modern art, including a few Warhol prints, a selection of Disney pieces, and even a framed picture of the Beatles, the *Abbey Road* record cover. She'd be sure to tell Moira to enquire about selling some of the works she'd produced while at college as part of her Fine Arts degree. It could be a nice little earner for her.

Up ahead, Maureen could see the photo boards they were looking for and, eager to see hers and Donal's, she quickened her pace. 'I'll start down this end. You start down there, Donal,' she bossed, patting about her person for her glasses.

'In the pocket of your caftan, Mo,' Donal said, pulling his own glasses from his shirt pocket.

'I'd be lost without you, so I would, Donal.'

They began scanning the boards with rows of identical cruise ship background photographs filled with smiling families, couples and groups, the minutes ticking by until she heard Donal mutter, 'Oh dear.'

'What's oh dear?' She moved alongside him, head tilted to one side as she studied the unfortunate shot of them both on display. Donal looked like he was chewing a wasp and she appeared startled, as though someone had jumped out at her.

This was the case because the photographer had leapt in front of her and she'd not had time to arrange herself into her photo pose, whereby she raised her chin just so. It took years off.

'I don't think it's one for the album Donal, do you?'

'I think you're right, Mo.'

It was just as well the children weren't here because they'd have a field day with it, Maureen thought. She'd warn Pat and the girls about the man floating about with the camera as you walked up the gangplank. 'Shall we carry on?'

Donal held his arm out for her to link by reply, then said, 'We're heading toward the Atrium area now. It's in the middle of the ship.'

The size of the ship was mind-boggling, Maureen thought happily, leaving the unfortunate photo behind in favour of the shops.

When they emerged in the glitzy, almost circular area overlooking the atrium floor below, passengers in various states of dress and undress were milling about, stocking up on duty-free, trying on jewellery, or eyeing nautical- or tropically-themed fashions. Maureen leaned over the railing, looking up at the enormous chandelier dangling overhead, then across to where the grand staircase swept down to the floor below where a woman was tinkling the ivories. People sat in bucket seats, sipping drinks from the nearby bar and coffee shop, enjoying the sophisticated ambience of it all. A glass elevator let passengers on and off, and the guest services area was tucked away in the corner where people were lined up waiting for assistance or booking shore excursions. They'd have to get on to that themselves, Maureen thought, eager to see what was on offer to explore their various cruise stops.

'I read on the programme sheet that there's a champagne waterfall in the atrium on the formal night. I'd like to see that. I hope it doesn't clash with our performance times.'

Donal was only half-listening as his toe began tapping to the Elton John number the woman had started playing. 'She's very good.' He hummed along to a few lines of 'Your Song', then pointed. 'Look, Niall's sitting over there.'

'Shall we ask if he minds us joining him? We could sit and listen for a while. I might request a bit of Richard Clayderman. I had a soft spot for him in the eighties. I found his music soothing when the girls and Pat tried my patience. The girls used to say, "You've done it now, Mammy's after putting the Richard Clayderman record on."' She'd liked his lovely blonde hair, too.

'Should I be jealous, Mo?' Donal's eyes twinkled.

'Not at all, Donal. I had an even bigger soft spot for Kenny Rogers!'

Linking arms again, they ventured downstairs.

Chapter 9

Life had taught Maureen a few things along the way, and something that never ceased to surprise her was how true the old saying about not being able to judge a book by its cover was. This was on her mind; sitting in her bucket seat between Niall and Donal, she stared at the woman flashing her audience an ear-to-ear smile now and again as her fingers banged up and down on the piano keys. The crowd she'd brought in with her lively rendition of Jerry Lee Lewis's 'Great Balls of Fire' were clapping along, and that was when it dawned on Maureen who the pianist was.

Carole from Australia. The stand-offish woman whom she'd met at the lift earlier. Although it was hard to believe this animated performer with the curled, bouncy hair and red lips was the same nondescript woman she'd tried and failed to engage in conversation. Maureen leaned over to Donal and shouted in his ear as to who the pianist was, but the rapt expression on Niall's face caught her attention. As the song ended, Carole thanked the crowd who'd gathered around and told them she'd be back after a short break.

'That was great altogether.' Niall's eyes were shining. 'The way her fingers flew over those keys.'

'Why don't you go up and say hello to her, Niall.' Maureen inclined her head to where Carole was pouring herself a glass of water from the jug on the bar. 'Tell her how much you enjoyed her set. Donal and I met her earlier. She's an Australian from Sydney, and her name's Carole.'

Niall morphed into a shy, fidgety teenager. 'Ah no, I'm heading back to the cabin now. I'll see you at seven.'

'Uh oh. You've got that look, Mo,' Donal said, clearly amused.

'And what look would that be?'

'That matchmaking look of yours.'

He knew her so well, Maureen thought with a smile, suggesting they head back to their cabin to freshen up before dinner.

Maureen would liken her first sighting of the Lido Buffet to standing in front of one of the manmade wonders of the earth: the Taj Mahal, perhaps, or the Great Wall of China. The buffet was a breathtaking spread of temptation and, leaving Donal to mind the table they'd found by the window, she set off in a daze with all her senses tingling. Did she fancy Asian or Mexican? A carvery or seafood? Oh, and the salads! There was every kind under the sun. As for the dessert counters, she'd investigate those later. There was so much choice Maureen was momentarily frozen with inertia, standing there with her nose twitching at all the delicious smells like a rabbit in a field sniffing for danger.

'It's hard to know where to start.' John, The Gamblers' drummer, mooched alongside her, startling Maureen from her food trance.

'That's not a problem Davey's having, I see.' Maureen's eyes flitted to where the keyboardist was loading his plate sky high and she laughed. 'I have to tell you, John, you're looking very smart in your chino trousers, so you are.' Maureen had noticed

John's get-up when they'd met him and the other two lads at the entrance to the Lido Buffet as arranged, but this was her first chance to compliment him.

'Thank you, Maureen. They were my daughter Breda's choice. She took me shopping for the cruise.'

'My girls and I did the same thing and your Breda's done you proud.'

John looked pleased. 'You know, I think I fancy roast pork. You can't beat a bit of crackling.'

'Go for your life, boyo!' He'd a definite swagger as he moved toward the carvery, resulting from her complimenting the chinos Maureen suspected. Her head swung this way and that to settle on soup. It seemed as good a starting point as any, so she ladled the chicken and corn broth into a bowl when Donal popped up alongside the tureen.

'You want to see the plate Davey's just sat down with, Mo.' Donal picked up a bowl himself. 'Chicken and corn sounds nice.'

'He's not the only one, Donal.' They glanced around and saw people carrying plates that must have been three times their usual portion size. 'I can see we're going to have to watch ourselves because if we don't show a degree of discipline we'll wind up the size of a bus by the time we head home.'

'You're not wrong there, Mo.' Donal, who'd picked up a set of tongs, put them back. 'I don't think I'll have a roll with my soup after all.'

'And I'll only have one dessert,' Maureen added.

They sealed the deal with a nod and then sanctimoniously carried their soup bowls, minus bread of any description, back to the table. Niall had joined them and was tucking into battered fish. It was agreed between the group of five that they'd landed on their feet with this gig aboard the *Mayan Princess*.

Maureen wished she had a roll to wipe up the remains of her soup when she saw Carole, the pianist, holding a plate while scanning the busy buffet restaurant for a table. Not one to miss an opportunity, her hand shot up. 'Yoo-hoo, Carole, over here.'

Carole tracked the source of the voice and frowned.

'I don't think she remembers you, Mo,' Donal said, spooning up the dregs of his soup.

Maureen was already out of her seat, oblivious to Niall slinking down in his. She bustled over to the bewildered woman and explained how they'd met briefly at the lifts earlier in the day, before gushing over her piano playing in the atrium and insisting she join them. 'We'll be fellow musos altogether like.' Maureen beamed.

If she didn't want to appear rude then Carole had no choice but to follow her over to the table.

'Bunch up next to Niall there,' Maureen bossed as subtle as a bull in a china shop before launching into a round of introductions. 'I was just telling Carole how much we enjoyed her set in the Atrium.'

'You were very good,' Niall said, a red flush creeping slowly up his neck. For a moment, Maureen thought she would have to stay put to ensure conversation at the table didn't peter out awkwardly because John and Davey were intent on eating like pigs at a trough. Then, to her surprise, Niall asked Carole if it was her first cruise ship gig; she was a newbie just like them.

'Who are you sharing your cabin with, Carole?' Davey asked, telling her about Kevin, the dry, Canadian comedian they were dossing down with.

'Three dancers from the shows in the Grand Theatre. One girl is from Brazil, the other two are Argentinian, and their English is as limited as my Spanish and Portuguese. It's strange sharing a room with strangers at my age. I haven't done that since my backpacking, hostel days.'

Maureen satisfied the ice was broken, looked to Donal. 'Shall we?'

'Don't mind if we do, Mo.'

Before they got up from the table, however, Maureen caught a glimpse of a white-clad, tanned fine figure of a fella striding through the restaurant. A hush fell over the tables, and heads turned in his wake.

'Look at yer Captain BeeGee acting the cock o' the walk, like,' Donal sniffed.

Maureen was thinking how well he'd look on the cover of one of those Mills and Boon books Rosemary Farrell enjoyed, in his Captain's uniform. However, she decided not to voice this, instead hauling Donal off to the buffet. 'The Asian cuisine looks interesting.' She eyed the black bean stir fry before glancing back at the table, delighted to see Niall and Carole in animated conversation. 'Well, would you look at that. Mark my words, Donal, tis a shipboard romance those two are headed for.'

'Wasn't the show something, Mo?' Donal said, emerging from the bathroom having finished his ablutions.

Maureen concurred, setting aside the newsletter she'd helped herself to from the guests' desk, having seen other passengers leafing through it. As employees aboard the ship, their copy wasn't slid under their cabin door each evening. Donal switched the light off, and the boxy room was plunged into total a blackout. 'Stay right where you are, Donal, and put that light back on. Sure, you could trip over and break your neck. It's so dark.'

Obediently Donal switched the light back on and pulled the bathroom door so he had a chink of light to guide him over to the bed.

'And the show was wonderful. I couldn't believe my eyes when Pawel made Tomasina vanish like that. Magic is what it was.'

'They were very clever, and wasn't it refreshing not to see any of that old pulling a rabbit out of a hat malarkey?'

'It was. I wonder if Tomasina will reveal any tricks of the trade. I don't fancy my chances getting Pawel to talk.'

'But Mo, that would ruin the magic.'

Maureen thought about that for a moment and decided he was right. 'You're a wise man, Donal McCarthy. Night, night.' They exchanged a kiss and settled in for the night. After a while, Maureen realised she could feel the gentle rise and fall of the boat over the waves, and she groaned.

'Are you alright, Mo?'

'I'm not feeling too clever, as it happens.'

'I didn't think you got seasick.'

Maureen could sense him frowning. 'I don't. It's the memory of all those desserts I ate.' There'd been cheesecake, pannacotta, a fruit tartlet, and chocolate brownie with a raspberry compote, with small portions of each, granted. Still, it was a rich combination now churning unhappily in her tummy. 'Why didn't you stop me after the pannacotta?'

'I didn't dare. You were like a woman possessed, Mo. No one was coming between you and the dessert counter, and I'd seen how you told that woman off who was helping herself to all the watermelon.'

'I was amid a sugar rush, Donal, and there was no need for yer woman to be so greedy.' A tad hypocritical, given her four servings of dessert. She kept that thought to herself. 'I dread what Aisling will be like when she sees the Lido Buffet's extensive dessert offerings. She'll be like your round one in the *Charlie and the Chocolate Factory* story, who didn't meet a good end. He fell into the Chocolate River from memory. Mind you, I can think of worst ways to go.'

'Stop thinking about the desserts. It won't make you feel any better.' Donal was quiet for a moment then, in what Maureen suspected was an attempt to distract her, said, 'Niall and

Carole seemed to get along well. You might be right about the shipboard romance.'

It worked because she forgot about her poor tummy, recalling how Niall and Carole had discovered a shared love of Captain and Tenille's music. 'They certainly did, Donal. Although she's a hard one to work out, is Carole.'

'What do you mean?'

'She went very quiet when I asked after her family.' Maureen couldn't understand why someone wasn't eager to chat about their nearest and dearest, especially when she'd just finished telling Carole all about her and Donal's children and their grandchildren, but Carole's expression had become guarded when Maureen had asked if she had children. She'd mumbled she had a daughter, and that had been the end of that.

Something was going on with Carole, and Maureen would get to the bottom of it because Niall's wife had let him down badly. Whomever he got involved with needed to be mindful of that. A person's heart was precious and needed to be handled with care. Maureen remembered something else then and groaned again. 'Donal, I wish we hadn't had the cheese, crackers and wine after dinner.'

'We'll be more disciplined tomorrow, Mo. Sure, it was the novelty of having it all there on offer. We were like children let loose in a sweet shop, so we were. In no time, we'll be like those folks who work at McDonald's and can't stand the burgers because they're sick of seeing them at the end of the day.'

Maureen found it very hard to believe she could ever get sick of cheesecake, pannacotta and chocolate. The fruit tart, however, she could take or leave.

Chapter 10

♥

Day 2 - At Sea

'Where am I, Donal?' Maureen opened her eyes into the inky room, confused and fuddly-headed.

Donal jolted awake and, ignoring the guilty twinge at having woken him, she asked again, not liking being so disorientated.

'In our cabin on the *Mayan Princess*, Mo.'

'Oh yes.' It all came back to Maureen in a rush. 'And what's the time?' she croaked. It was a disconcerting thing being in a ship's cabin below decks without so much as a porthole to give you a clue whether it was day or night. Donal must have turned the bathroom light he'd left on out in the night.

Donal yawned and stretched before flicking on the bedside light and picking up his watch. 'It's gone eight, Mo.'

'Gone eight!' She pulled herself upright and then wished she hadn't.

'Yes. Does it matter?'

'It does, actually.' Maureen didn't mean to sound snippy, but she wasn't a good patient and, at this moment, needed some TLC. 'I wanted to go to the sunrise yoga session on the Lido deck to tell Roisin whether it was any cop when I emailed the girls my cruise ship life update, tomorrow.' Maureen had selected the activities on offer today from the 'At Sea' newsletter as she had waited for Donal to finish his ablutions last night. Nothing in their contract said they couldn't take part in things between gigs, and she thought it would be a case of the more the merrier. The Margherita-making class had grabbed her attention, and she'd been about to mention it to Donal when she read the small print. It wasn't complimentary. Still, seeing there was to be a pub quiz made up for it. Maureen loved a good pub quiz and prided herself on her knowledge of films, which usually saw her team sweep the floor with the others. Although, to be fair, she thought massaging her poor temples, she wasn't feeling too sharp this morning and might have to give it a miss.

Maureen knew why she was feeling rough. She'd been here before. It was a sugar hangover. Self-inflicted maybe, but she knew she could count on Donal for sympathy. So, what he said next didn't impress her.

'Ah sure, never mind, Mo. There's always tomorrow for the yoga,' Donal said cheerily. He added, 'And if you like, we could go to the gym before breakfast.'

Maureen stared at him, aghast. Who was this man sharing her bed? She shook her head.

'Silly idea?'

'Very.'

'It's a shame there's no kitchenette because I like a cup of tea first thing in the morning, as you know,' Donal lamented.

'I'd murder a coffee,' Maureen said wistfully.

'Shall we get showered and dressed then and see what we can find?'

'I'll go first.' Maureen tossed the covers off and staggered forth to the teeny-tiny bathroom.

CHAPTER 10

'Are you feeling delicate, Maureen?' Niall, spreading jam on his toast, paused to squint up at Maureen.

She and Donal had spotted the three lads when they'd emerged from the lift without incident this morning and wandered out into the glorious sunshine hinting at the hot day ahead. They were enjoying an alfresco breakfast on the Lido deck. At the same time, nearby, a couple sucked on cigarettes like their life depended on it, and already children's heads were bobbing in the pool water. The music playing wasn't as boisterous as it had been yesterday afternoon, and laughter and chatter could be heard over the top of it. The atmosphere was very convivial, Maureen thought, not feeling very convivial herself.

'One too many, was it?' Davey asked, hoovering up eggs, beans, sausage and bacon.

'Hair of the dog's what you need by the looks of those enormous sunglasses you've on, Maureen. Bar's open.' John, who'd already cleaned his plate up and was reclining in his chair, gestured to the bar and cast a wistful eye toward the smokers.

Maureen pulled a face, wondering what, aside from her Jackie O sunglasses, had given her away. Her slow gait and slumped shoulders perhaps? 'I didn't overdo it as it happens, lads. Well, I did, but not on the sauce as you're implying.' She pushed her sunglasses onto her head, blinking at the brightness of the sunshine and sea. A sudden piercing child's squeal followed by a splash saw her wince. 'It's a sugar crash I'm suffering from.'

'What's that when it's home?' Davey asked, mopping up his egg yolk with a piece of toast.

'The terrible low that follows the high after a sugar rush, Davey. It's thanks to all those desserts I put away after dinner. It's as bad as a hangover, and I don't mind telling you I'm suffering for my sins today, so I am.'

All three men looked at Maureen like she'd suddenly grown two heads.

'It's a thing,' she insisted, looking to Donal for backup.

'Tossed and turned all night she has, lads, moaning and groaning about cheesecake and the likes being the work of the divil,' he said in a jolly voice before announcing he fancied an omelette. A portable cooking station was in hot demand near the bar where several chefs were earning their keep frying them in the open air.

'Would you mind getting me one, Donal?' Maureen sank into the spare seat at the table like the maiden in distress.

'Not at all. It might sort you out.' Donal headed off to join the queue.

'I'll fetch you a coffee,' Niall said putting his toast down. 'You look like you need one.'

'That's very kind of you, Niall.' Maureen, whose energy levels were as low as an empty petrol tank, couldn't be arsed telling him to finish his toast first.

John watched his pal go and, as he disappeared inside the restaurant, said, 'Niall and yer Carole woman seemed to hit it off last night.'

'They did. I never knew Niall was a Captain and Tenille fan.' To be fair, there was no reason she should have.

'Someone has to be,' John said.

'Now, now, John, the "Love Will Keep Us Together" song was very catchy,' Davey piped up.

John sighed. 'Don't mind me.' He looked longingly at the spirals of smoke rising above the nearby couple's heads.

'You've done so well knocking it on the head, John,' Maureen reminded him gently.

'It's mad how you can crave something you know is bad for you.' John was hypnotised by the smoke spiralling into the sky.

If she'd had the energy, Maureen would have gone over and asked if they had to make such a show of enjoying things because there was a man at her table who'd given up but was

CHAPTER 10   65

sorely tested. Sure, the self-satisfied expressions as they blew the smoke out would have you thinking they were postcoital. She wasn't in good form, she thought, muttering, 'Tell me about it.' The cheesecake and its sweet partners in crime she'd over-indulged in sprang to mind.

'The proof in the pudding was it, Maureen?' Davey piped up, thinking himself hilarious. He was close to wheezing as he added, 'You know what they say, "You are what you eat".'

Maureen gave him her most withering look. He'd a peculiar sense of humour, did Davey. She was grateful when Niall returned with a much-needed mug of coffee for her. He'd even remember she liked a dash of milk, which surprised and pleased her. 'Thanks a million, Niall.' He shot up in her favourite member of The Gamblers rankings. Of course, Donal held the number one position.

Carole would be a lucky woman if she and Niall were to get together, Maureen thought. She'd made the assumption the pianist was single given her three-month solo contract. It was a long time to be away from a partner. Single or not, she was getting ahead of herself as he set a mug down for Donal, too. She let the galvanising effects of caffeine work their magic as she sipped her drink, sparing a glance over at the omelette station. Seeing Donal being accosted by a red-headed woman – the hair wasn't natural, Maureen's hawk-eye deduced – her gaze narrowed. The redhead was thrusting a paper napkin and pen at him while Donal, holding his hands up like he was under arrest, shook his head at her. If Maureen had had the energy to do so, she'd march over and tell your woman there Donal was a retiree from Ireland. It was both a curse and a blessing to bear such a close resemblance to Kenny Rogers.

'Here we are, Mo. Get that down you, and you'll be a new woman.' Donal returned a few minutes later unscathed and slid a plain cheese omelette under her nose.

'I saw your woman up there with the red hair,' she said after thanking him. Then, inspecting her omelette, she gave the chef a ten out of ten for presentation. The garnish of parsley sprinkled over the golden, cheesy egg dish was a nice touch.

'Ah, sure, it took some doing to convince her I wasn't Kenny taking a break from my new album with a Mexican Riviera cruise.' Donal searched for a spare chair, pulling one up and sitting down to enjoy his breakfast.

'How'd you manage it in the end?' John asked, relaxing now your smoking couple had stubbed their cigarettes out.

'I told her to come to the Havana Lounge this evening, and she'd see for herself that I'm the singer in a tribute band.'

'Good man, drumming up business,' John said approvingly. He'd once confided that after a lacklustre sixtieth wedding anniversary gig, his greatest fear was performing a live show and looking out to the audience to see there was no one there.

'Well, just so long as she doesn't try to do a "Jolene" on me. She's got the flamin locks, after all.' Maureen was only half-teasing as she asked what colour eyes she'd had.

'They weren't emerald green, Maureen, and I've only eyes for you.'

Maureen smiled as she added a sprinkle of salt to her omelette. A companionable silence fell across the table as Maureen and Donal ate, and the others watched the world go by. By the time she set her knife and fork down and drained her mug, the brain fog she'd woken with was beginning to lift and she decided she would be alright to take part in the 11am pub quiz after all. At least she could tick something off the 'At Sea' newsletter.

Donal wiped his mouth then balled the napkin, dropped it on his plate and said, 'I'm going to put my name down for the table tennis tournament this afternoon. Are any of you keen to help me train?'

'You know my views on couples and competitive sport, Donal. The two don't mix,' Maureen said sagely, silently debating a second coffee even though she'd need the loo every five minutes for the rest of the day if she pushed the boat out and went for it.

'I'm not asking you to play a game with me. Just lob the ping-pong over the net, Mo.'

'No, Donal. Have you forgotten the incident at the Howth community centre? You snapped the bat when you threw it down in a temper the last time we were "practising".' She made the inverted commas with her fingers.

'It's a paddle, Mo,' Donal said because of the lack of any other comeback.

'Don't look at me,' Davey and Niall said in tandem, but John put his hand up, saying, 'I'll do it, but you'll owe me one of those Blue Lagoon cocktails. I'm not a cocktail man, but those were very nice.'

'Done,' Donal replied.

'There's a pub quiz at eleven this morning in the Sundowner Bar. Would any of you like to make up a team?'

'I can't stand pub quizzes.' John was quick off the mark.

'Just as well, pal, because you'll be busy training with me for the tournament,' Donal informed him, making a swishing motion as though he already had a paddle in his hand.

'So you're out too, Donal?'

'I'm sorry, Mo, but the table tennis has to come first.'

Maureen pursed her lips but decided to let it go. You had to pick your battles when you were in a relationship. As such, she turned to the two remaining lads, hopefully. 'Davey, Niall?'

'Ah, g'won then,' Davey said, eyeing the contents of a plate passing by. 'I didn't see those chocolate pastry yokes. One of those would round things off nicely.' He scraped his chair back.

'Niall?'

'Count me in, Maureen.'

'Grand.' Feeling pleased, Maureen decided she would have that second coffee and, taking orders, padded off into the restaurant. 'Fancy meeting you here,' she said tongue in cheek, seeing Carole dipping a teabag in and out of a mug. By the end of a week onboard the ship, Maureen suspected they'd all feel like they were guest starring in that Australian soap opera that made the Minogue girl famous. She'd a lot to answer for did the Minogue girl, in Maureen's opinion, because she'd seen the hotpants video for that catchy pop tune a few years back. As soon as the song caught on, Moira, a sheep when it came to following fashion, wanted a pair of teeny-tiny gold shorts. They'd had words with Maureen, saying she could spin around in the things all she liked so long as she didn't leave the privacy of her own home. Maureen blinked her youngest child and her habit of taking things too far away. Instead she focussed on Carole, who gave her a wan smile. *Was she suffering from a sugar hangover, too?* Maureen wondered before saying, 'The omelettes they're serving on the deck out there are delicious, so they are.'

'I've already eaten.'

'Oh.' *She was hard work was Carole,* Maureen thought, chattering on about her family while they waited for the tea to brew. 'Sure mine and Donal's life is busier than a fiddler's arm since the grandchildren came along.' This was Carole's cue to step in a tell her a little of her life but nothing was forthcoming. Maureen, who couldn't stand awkward silences, thought about mentioning the Captain and Tenille music but decided against it. Sure, what relevance did they have at the tea and coffee station? Then, remembering the pub quiz, she brightened. 'Are you free around elevenish this morning, Carole?'

The Australian woman looked cagey, but Maureen was well used to that look from her girls and carried on unperturbed. 'Only there's a pub quiz in the Sundowner lounge. Myself, Davey and Niall will be there,' she added coyly. 'You'd be very welcome.'

To her amazement, Carole replied, 'You know, Maureen, I think I'll take you up. I could do with a distraction.'

From what? Maureen wondered, but Carole had already dropped her tea bag in the rubbish bin and was walking away.

Chapter 11

♥

'What about the Captain and the Tenilles?' Carole suggested, the curls from last night escaping the loose bun she'd pulled her hair back into since Maureen had seen her at breakfast. The foursome had gathered as arranged in the Sundowner Lounge and were now trying to come up with a name for their quiz team. So far, all suggestions had been vetoed as unoriginal or not applicable. The slow nodding around the table suggested Carole had come up with a winner. The final vote rested with Maureen, however, as self-appointed team leader.

'Very good, Carole,' Maureen said, thinking there was no need to clarify who the Captain in the name was. '"Captain and the Tenilles" it is.'

Everybody looked pleased, especially Carole who smiled and sat up straighter as she smoothed the creases in her simple linen dress. Maureen thought she should smile more often because it lit up her eyes and transformed her from someone you might not notice to someone you'd like to sit down and chat with.

Over by the bar, the *Mayan Princess*'s toothy Director of Entertainment was testing her microphone. Maureen leaned over to Carole and whispered, 'Your woman up there, Christie, has one of those terrible, annoying swingy ponytails.'

CHAPTER 11

Carole looked to see Christie's ponytail was indeed swinging and whispered back, 'You're right. It's the sort of ponytail that would be super satisfying to snip off.'

They grinned at one another. It was a grin that said two women who didn't know each other well had found a surprising kindred spirit.

'To be fair, she's very enthusiastic,' Maureen said because she prided herself on being fair.

'Albeit a tad shouty,' Carole added.

'With a look of Mr Ed's talking horse about her,' Maureen couldn't help herself.

'I remember that! "A horse is a horse—"' "Of course,' Maureen finished.

The menfolk looked at the women as they collapsed in giggles and shook their heads.

'Women are a mysterious lot,' Davey said to Niall as if he'd had loads of experience on the matter.

Once she'd recovered, Maureen asked around their group whether they should disclose to Christie that they were crew. The general consensus was: what difference would it make? So she donned her captain's hat, figuratively speaking, and glanced around the Sundowner lounge to see the tables were filling up. She sized up the competition and then drilled her teammates on where their strengths lay, suggesting they envisage the game of Trivial Pursuit with its pieces of pie for the correct answers.

'I sweep the floor, winning all the blue pie slices for the geography questions,' Davey said.

Maureen looked to Niall. 'And yourself?'

'I'm an orange pie man myself. You know, sports and leisure.'

'Grand, grand,' Maureen said, crossing her toes under the table in her sandals, that Carole wasn't a pink pie girl because entertainment was her forte. She uncrossed them as cramp was swift to settle in.

'Brown pie. Arts and Literature,' Carole said.

Maureen could have kissed her. 'And I'm the queen of entertainment questions. It sounds like we're a well-rounded team with all our bases covered. So c'mon, Tennilles. Let's wipe the floor with this lot!' Maureen said, picking up her pen and paper to write down their answers. They all looked attentively to where Christie was beginning her welcome and general housekeeping spiel. Davey was shaking his hands like he was limbering up for a jog, which was as likely as Maureen suddenly deciding that Daniel Day-Lewis's *The Last of the Mohicans* wasn't the best film ever made.

'Get on with it,' Maureen muttered for fear Davey would get up and start doing hamstring stretches or the like.

Finally, Christie started with a question that saw them all smile in that 'I know this one' way. 'What year did the *Titanic* sink on its maiden voyage?'

Only it turned out they didn't know.

'History, who is our history buff?' Maureen glanced around the table, but no one put their hand up. It seemed they had all their bases covered *except* history. 'I know it was in the early 1900s. I'm thinking 1920.'

'I feel it was more like 1910,' Davey volunteered.

'Yes, that sounds familiar.' Niall was nodding, as was Carole.

Maureen went with the majority and jotted down 1910.

The next question was easy. 'What is the smallest country in the world by land area?'

'Liechtenstein!' Davey announced jubilantly.

'And you call yourself a good Catholic boy.' Maureen shook her head. 'It's the Vatican, you eejit.'

'Oh yes.' Davey was chastened as he gazed heavenward and muttered a 'Sorry about that'.

As the questions were fired, Maureen noticed the woman leaning toward them at the closest table to theirs. She beckoned Niall, Davey and Carole closer for a quick pow-wow.

CHAPTER 11 73

'Watch your wan there in the pink pantsuit. She's flapping ears, so she has.'

By the sixth question, the Captain and Tenilles were slumping, dejected in their seats. The lads were tense with the prospect of defeat, and Niall had told Davey he was as useful as a one-legged man in an arse-kicking competition. Christie's questions became increasingly cryptic, and none of their team was a fan of the cryptic crossword.

Maureen decided a team pep talk was in order at half-time. Once Davey had finished complaining that the *Titanic* question was a bit on the nose, given they were on a big ship in the middle of the ocean, she said, 'Alright, so, Tenilles, listen up. What's in the past has been and gone. I want you to cast the first round from your minds because we can claw victory back from the jaws of defeat.' She made claws of her hands to demonstrate. 'And let's not lose perspective here. It's a quiz. It's supposed to be fun; we're here to enjoy ourselves. Right?' She didn't mean a word of it. She was here to win.

Davey fist-pumped the air. 'Right!' Startled heads spun their way and he lowered his arm. 'Sorry, but you're very good at this, Maureen. You could have been one of those motivational speakers.'

'Oh, do you think so?'

'I do.'

'I think Davey's got a point,' Niall said.

'I was feeling like throwing the towel in, Maureen, to be honest, but now I'm rearing to go,' Carole added.

Maureen was pleased and filed away motivational speaker as a new part-time career avenue to explore further once the littlest grandchildren started school and her services weren't in such hot demand. She might be retired but she far from out to pasture and sure she might enjoy doing the rounds of Dublin spreading her words of wisdom!

Then, remembering she was amid a pep talk, she said, 'Tenilles, win or lose – but obviously winning would feel loads better – we're a team, and we've got this. No fist pumps, please, Davey. Okay, deep breaths, everybody.' Maureen thought a spot of the pranayama breathing Roisin swore by might help clear their minds and prepare them for round two. She was about to demonstrate the technique when Christie picked up the mic again.

Twenty-five minutes later, Niall placed a restraining hand on Maureen's arm. She was all set to march over to Christie and tell her she suspected the winning team, the Quizzards of Oz, of cheating because she'd seen the pink pantsuit lady just about dislocating her neck trying to read the answers of the Smarty Pints team at the table behind hers. 'Sure, look at her all smug like with her *Mayan Princess* plastic drink bottle. I've got her number. She's the sort if you were to say you were off to Tenerife, she'd reply she was off to Elevenerife.'

Carole snorted.

'We've to be graceful in defeat,' Niall was saying. 'Although I might have a word with Christie myself because the sporting questions were very one-eyed, so they were. It was all baseball, basketball and football. What's an Irishman supposed to know about any of that? Some hurling questions next time would even the playing field out.' He released his grip on Maureen's arm to explain to Carole what hurling was.

Davey looked at Maureen and huffed, 'I think that question about what sort of a country sounds like it should be cold but actually isn't was ridiculous. I mean, I had a very temperate holiday in Vancouver, Canada, years back, and you can't tell me it's not fecking cold in Iceland.' He drained his pint, thumping it down on the table.

'We should have known the *Titanic* went down in 1912.' Niall moved on from his hurling monologue to Carole.

'Don't mention the *Titanic* when we're on a fecking boat!' Davey's voice rose.

Maureen knew that, as captain, she should calm the fraught atmosphere and give them ten out of ten for effort. If she were

CHAPTER 11

Captain Franco, she'd tell them in his hot chocolate voice it wasn't the winning that mattered but how you played the game, only she couldn't bring herself to. The winning did matter; the *Mayan Princess*'s drink bottle would be indispensable for the sunrise yoga session. Then again, as crew, was she allowed to accept free merchandise? It was a question that would have to wait to be answered another day because Davey was rubbing his belly with one hand and glancing at his watch strapped to the other wrist.

'Well, would you look at that? It's lunchtime. Shall we mosey up to the buffet?' he suggested.

Niall and Carole said they'd go with Davey but Maureen said she'd wander out to see how John and Donal were getting on and see if she could drag them off the table tennis table for a spot of lunch.

'Good luck with that,' Niall said.

Maureen felt she would need it because Donal was like a man possessed when he got that ping-pong bat in his hand.

Chapter 12

♥

Maureen was alone in the lift for the few floors to the Lido Deck, where Donal was practising his ping-pong with John. Then the doors slid open, and the sinewy manchild from London's East End or somewhere nearby stepped in. She'd almost not recognised him dressed in civvies. His tights and tank top had been swapped for shorts and a t-shirt. If he recognised her as the woman he'd given short shrift to along with her manfriend in the Grand Theatre yesterday, he wasn't letting on.

He'd been unnecessarily rude, Maureen thought, wondering if he could feel her eyes boring into his back. The bubbling volcano sensation saw her begin crooning 'We've Got Tonight' softly, for reasons she didn't understand. However, she was gratified seeing his shoulders tense. *Ha*, she thought: he knew who she was now alright and had a guilty conscience. When the doors opened on the eleventh floor, he shot off so fast she fancied she could smell the burning rubber of his flip-flops. *Served him right*, she thought, pulling her sunglasses down from the top of her head as she emerged into the sunshine.

Maureen weaved her way around the deck chairs littered about the pool. They were all taken by people who were either slurping drinks, reading books, or sleeping under the hot sun. She spied a sensible woman slathering sunscreen on and thought there'd be a run on the E45 cream in the pharmacy this afternoon when the other eejits baking themselves sought relief from their sunburn.

The table tennis tables were set up in a sheltered area, undercover behind one of the bars and near the entrance to the spa and gym. She could see Donal down one end of a table, John the other. She rolled her eyes because despite Donal having his back to her, she could see him bouncing on his toes and passing the paddle from hand to hand like a tennis pro while waiting for John to serve the ping-pong ball.

The other table was in use, and several small children with fed-up expressions were milling about. As she drew nearer, she heard one child saying, 'I'm going to tell my dad they won't get off the table and let us have a turn.'

'Donal!' Maureen called out. Donal swung around hearing his name and promptly missed the serve John sent.

A little girl quickly picked the ping-pong ball up as it bounced on the deck.

'Mo. Don't shout my name out like that during the tournament later.'

Donal was uncharacteristically snappy, and Maureen blamed the paddle he had a death-like grip on. He was holding his left hand out for the ball, but the little girl wasn't handing it over.

'My mommy says sharing is caring, Mister, and you're not letting anyone else have a turn playing.'

'But I'm training for a tournament. I'm not messing about. Would your mammy tell your man Agassi to get off the court when Wimbledon was looming? Now give me that ball.'

'Donal, get a grip.' Maureen's tone matched his in the snappiness stakes. 'Enough. She's only a child, and the passengers are king, remember?'

'I tried telling him, Maureen.' John had put his paddle down and come around the table to where she stood with her hands on her hips. 'It went in one ear and out the other though.'

'What are you doing, John? The tournament's in a few hours. I need to work on my backhand.' Donal's gaze swung wildly from the child with the ping-pong ball to his bandmate.

'Donal McCarthy, put that bat on the table now or I'll be working on *my* backhand.'

'My mommy also says we talk with this.' The little girl put her index finger to her mouth and then raised a fist. 'Not with this.'

Maureen was beginning to think this child's mammy would be a very annoying woman altogether and, ignoring her, she changed tact with Donal.

'Donal, c'mere to me now. It's lunchtime, and you know you'll have no energy for the tournament without sustenance. Let the poor children have a turn on the table and come and have something to eat.'

Donal was torn, and Maureen watched the internal battle on his face.

'Well, I'm starving. I'll see you in the Lido Buffet.' John headed off.

Maureen held her hand out for the paddle as a hostage negotiator would a gun. 'There's no need for this sort of carry-on. Donal, remember the children's parents are paying guests. The table and the bats will be here after lunch.'

'I am a little peckish, and it's a paddle, not a bat, Mo.'

'The bat, paddle, whatever, Donal,' Maureen reminded him and, after a beat of hesitation, he passed it over to her. Just like that, Maureen had the Donal she knew and loved back. 'There you go. That wasn't so hard now, was it?' She gave the paddle to the little girl waiting for a turn, and Donal said she'd better make the most of the hour she had to play before he returned.

CHAPTER 12

The Lido Buffet restaurant was a seething mass of hungry cruise ship passengers piling plates up from the dazzling selection of dishes and then hunting out tables to sit and enjoy their meal. Donal had seemed to manage to put the upcoming tournament out of his mind and enjoy his leisurely lunch, Maureen thought, patting her mouth with her napkin before announcing to the group seated around the table that Niall, Davey and Carole had commandeered earlier, 'Variety is the spice of life. I thoroughly enjoyed my Mexican, Italian and Chinese lunch choices.'

'That lemon chicken was delicious,' Carole said, aware Maureen had had the same.

'It was, Carole,' Maureen agreed.

'I'm off to check out what's on offer for dessert,' Davey heaved himself up. 'Anybody care to join me?'

'Not me, Davey,' Maureen said piously.

'I spied lemon meringue pie earlier,' John announced, getting up.

Maureen's mouth watered. She loved lemon meringue pie.

'That's one of your favourites.' Donal got to his feet. 'Would you like me to get you a slice while I'm at it, Mo?'

'Just a teeny-tiny sliver like, Donal, thanks. Don't overdo it yourself; remember, you've got to be nimble on your feet this afternoon.'

'I won't, Mo,' he reassured her, stampeding off to the tempting lineup of treats.

Niall offered to get in a round of tea and coffee, leaving Maureen and Carole alone at the table.

'Thanks for including me this morning, Maureen. It was fun.'

Maureen smiled. 'You're very welcome, although it would have been more fun if we'd won the quiz. That *Mayan Princess* drink bottle would have been just the ticket for keeping Donal hydrated at this afternoon's tournament.'

'Yes, I suppose it would have been.'

She had a lovely, soft accent. Maureen thought more Olivia Newton-John than yer criminal wans in that *Prisoner Cell Block H* programme the girls had always begged to stay up late to watch. 'It must have been hard leaving your daughter for three months. My girls were bereft at thinking of Donal and me being away at sea for three months. Of course, treating them to an all-expenses holiday in a month aboard the *Mayan Princess* took the sting out of it for them.'

Carole smiled. 'Yes, I'd imagine it would have. So they're all coming?'

'What you do for one you have to do for all with my lot, and Donal's girls and their families are coming too.' She explained the unexpected windfall that had come Donal's way and how he'd generously decided to share it with all the family.

'How lovely to have them all together like so.'

'It will be, although we'll need eyes in the back of our heads on the ship with Noah and the toddler Kiera. They're dynamos, the pair of them, when they get together. I don't mind telling you the kids club staff will earn their money that week.' Maureen noticed Carole hadn't answered her question, so she asked it again: 'You must miss your daughter when you're away?'

Carole gave a slight nod but didn't meet Maureen's inquisitive eye as she picked up the salt cellar and inspected it.

'Does she have a family of her own? Grandchildren are such a blessing, like.'

'Not yet.'

This was like getting blood out of a stone, Maureen thought, but she'd cracked tougher nuts than Carole before. 'Is she a musician like yourself?'

'Yes, she is. She plays the piano too, but she's far more talented than I am.'

'I find that hard to believe. I've heard you play, remember? You'd give Richard Clayderman a run for his money any day. But it must be nice to have a chip off the old block. My

CHAPTER 12   81

children are nothing like me.' Maureen smiled. 'For one thing, they've not got a musical bone in their bodies. Not that we didn't encourage them, Bryan and I, that's my late husband. But there's only so much murdering of the recorder you can take. The toddler Kiera is showing great potential with the drums, though. She's got natural rhythm.' Maureen could see she'd lost Carole, who was staring out to sea. 'Are you alright there, Carole?'

'Mmm, sorry, what were you saying?'

Maureen decided to let things be where Carole's daughter was concerned for the time being. 'I was just saying how you and Niall seem to have hit it off.'

Carole smiled. 'He seems a nice man. It's not every day I meet a fellow Captain and Tenille fan.'

'No, I'd imagine not, and he's one of the good ones, is Niall.'

'Did I hear my name?' Niall appeared at the table with cups in either hand.

'I was talking about you, not to you.' Maureen accepted the brew with a thank you.

'But it was all good.' Carole smiled at him as she took her cuppa.

Maureen scanned the bustling corridor between tables and food stations for Donal, spotting him heading back to the table with his hands full. Maureen thought his idea of teeny-tiny and hers were two very different things, not complaining as she tucked into a generous wedge of lemon meringue pie he set down in front of her. Carole decided the pie looked too delicious not to partake, as did Niall. The pair of them went off to get themselves a serving, passing Davey who was grinning from ear to ear: in his happy place.

'I think I've died and gone to heaven,' he said, sitting down to enjoy his pudding.

The minutes ticked by as they ate silently, savouring the sweet treats and enjoying the never-ending vista of blue. It was beautiful, Maureen thought as Donal set his fork down and began twirling his hands around.

'Donal, watch out, you almost smacked poor Davey.'

'Sorry, Davey, but I'm limbering my wrists up.' Time had marched on, and there were only fifty minutes to go until the tournament was due to start. John had made it clear that Donal was on his own because he'd not be returning to the ping-pong table to help him practise, and nobody else had put their hand up to help. 'If I'm not getting back on the table between now and kick-off, then this will have to do.' He got up from the table and did a few calf stretches.

When the others returned with their desserts, they agreed to head over to the table tennis tables once they'd all finished.

Maureen and Donal found a small crowd was gathering and the children had been moved on, leaving the tables empty. Christie, who'd been in charge of the pub quiz, checked players off the enrolment form she'd attached to a clipboard. A sun visor was on her head but her ponytail was still swishing back and forth, putting Maureen in mind of a horse's tail swatting flies. Dodging it as it swished her way, she tapped the cruise ship's Director of Entertainment on the shoulder. 'Excuse me, Christie.'

'Hey there, are you playing in the tournament?'

'No. Donal is. Yer man over there doing the wrist twirls and lunges. I wanted to check in with you as to whether crew members are allowed to win prizes and, if so, is he playing for the chance to win a *Mayan Princess* drink bottle?'

'It is one of the prizes, yes, and so long as you don't play Bingo or participate in any games with a monetary prize, we can let the drink bottle go. Besides, they're so useful.' Christie's grin mesmerised Maureen and, for a moment, she thought she'd said, 'All the better to eat you up with!' ss the wolf who'd dressed up as grandma in Little Red Riding Hood sprang to mind. The bubbling volcano sensation starting up in her stomach was a welcome distraction from the Director of

Entertainment's gnashers, and she wondered whether it was due to the Mexican, Chinese and Italian food she'd not long ago enjoyed. No, she decided. It was down to the urgent need for Donal to win the tournament and take home the prize of a *Mayan Princess* drink bottle.

It was time to take action, and she needed to get behind him. So, telling him to stand still, Maureen began massaging his shoulders. She'd seen the managers of prize fighters sitting in the ring about to start punching the living daylights out of the other fella doing this in the boxing. If it worked for them, it would work for Donal. 'You've got this, Donal,' she said, eying his competitors milling about. She decided yer woman, who she put at around eighty-something years and who'd pulled her navy blue slacks up under her armpits, was the one to watch. She'd brought her own bat in a special case, no less.

Donal bounced from foot to foot when Maureen finished her pep talk and punched the air. 'You're very good at motivational speaking, so you are, Mo.'

'Thank you, Donal. You're not the first to tell me that, as it happens.'

Then, seeing the man with Bat Woman pass her a *Mayan Princess* drink bottle, Maureen knew this woman was a winner.

She thought the lady had better watch out because so was her Donal.

Chapter 13

Maureen was hiding beneath her sunhat and sunglasses, wearing her caftan over her swimsuit as she slunk into The Retreat. She'd a bag containing sunscreen and E45 cream because you never knew when you might need them, and she'd picked up a book at the airport bookshop. This was her first chance to open it. She'd fully intended to dive into the bestseller on the flight from Dublin to LA but was easily distracted, and there'd been too much going on. The introductions to their travel companions seated across the way, in front and behind, for one thing. By the time they were all on a first-name basis, the meal was being served, and lovely it was, too. Herself and Donal greatly enjoyed the cheese and crackers with a complimentary glass of wine. Of course, it was essential to keep the circulation going, so she'd headed to the back of the plane for a round of lunges, leaving Donal to his film. Before she'd known it, the seatbelt sign had come on for landing.

Now, she planned to lose herself in the pages, whiling away a few hours reading, getting swept up in someone else's fictional drama, and perhaps taking a dip in that invitingly blue water. Exhausted after the table tennis match, Donal had opted to relax back at the cabin. He knew where to find her later. The other lads had said they would hunt down the hay bales for the show in the Havana Lounge later and get it set up. Maureen had wished them luck but had no intention of helping. She needed to keep a low profile for the next few hours, and carting hay bales about the ship would not be conducive.

Her reason for venturing into the adults-only pool and bar area had nothing to do with wanting peace away from the squeals of exuberant youngsters – that was a sound she didn't mind in the least as a nana – but came back to the business of keeping a low profile after the ping-pong match shenanigans. Shenanigans she fervently hoped wouldn't reach the ears of Captain Franco because, for a while there, she'd lost her head and forgotten she was crew, as had Donal.

Things hadn't gone well for them and she felt like she'd a sign pinned to her back that said, 'When Ping-Pong Goes Bad.' Suppose the girls knew their mammy and Donal had received a lifetime ban from the table tennis tables aboard the *Mayan Princess*? In that case, she'd never hear the end of it. They'd not be hearing it from her. Her lips were sealed on the subject. Sure, hadn't she been telling Noah just a few weeks ago about the importance of being a good sport when he'd taken the modified hurling with the softball to the next level? Today, she hadn't led by example.

It was Christie, the Director of Entertainment, who'd slapped them with the ban, saying Maureen's behaviour was conducive to inciting violence which, as a crew member, was utterly unacceptable. While Donal had knowingly and wilfully destroyed cruise property. Maureen strongly suspected Christie might be a law school dropout.

She sighed, picking up a striped towel from the pile reserved for the pool area, casting about for an empty sun-lounger in a shady spot. She supposed they were lucky Christie was a Kenny Rogers fan and had decided to keep the matter in-house or on deck or whatever. Basically, she'd said she wouldn't take things higher up the cruise food chain on the condition Maureen and Donal gave the table tennis tables a wide berth for the duration of their natural lives and that The Gamblers played her favourite Kenny song, 'Daytime Friends', dedicating it to the Director of Entertainment whenever they played in the Havana Bar. Despite getting off relatively lightly, the whole episode had been traumatic, made worse by an overheard commentary about her from the sinewy, Eastend manchild. Oh, how she wished she could wipe it from her memory like that yoke Noah could draw on and then zip-zap the slate clean.

Spotting a lounger that would do her nicely, she passed by the busy bar area where people were relaxing at tables. Mercifully, they were too busy whiling away a lazy afternoon drinking in the sunshine to notice a sheepish Irish woman in a big hat skulking past. Maureen negotiated the sprawl of loungers, clearing her throat loudly as she passed by an amorous, bronzed couple squeezed onto one sunbed. *The pair looked like someone had drizzled a bottle of cooking oil over them*, she sniped silently. *Sprinkle salt and pepper on them, toss them on the barbeque, and Bob's your uncle*, she thought. Her lips pressed together because the woman's string bikini bottoms looked like they'd have to be surgically removed at some point. *Note to self,* she thought, *be sure to tell the girls that the ship enforced a strict swimwear code.* She mentally wrote down: *the bikini must cover the bottom at all times*. A complete fib, of course, but given her current mood, she didn't care.

Maureen was disgruntled and mortified, to say the least. Not a good combination and, flapping the towel out like she was battling gale-force winds, she lay it over the sunbed and settled herself in for the next few hours. Instead of opening her book, however, Maureen decided the pranayama breathing would help lift her mood. It was a shame to be in foul humour when she shouldn't have a care in the world. As such, she put her all into a round of controlled breathing exercises.

CHAPTER 13   87

She was concentrating intensely on her inhale of four counts when a voice made her lose her place.

'Ma'am, are you alright?'

Maureen blew out through her mouth in a noisy whoosh, lowering her glasses to peer over the top of the chunky black frames.

A young man in the ship's hospitality staff uniform, polo shirt tucked into a pair of smart shorts, was bending down to pick up the glass with nothing but melting ice cubes floating in the bottom alongside a nearby lounger.

'I'm grand, thank you very much.' She hoped she didn't sound short, but he'd interrupted her flow.

'It's just I get the asthma too. Mostly in winter, which isn't a problem on this cruise route, but it played up when I was working the Alaska itinerary. Anyway, I always keep an emergency inhaler on hand.' He held out a blue Ventolin puffer. 'I've another one back in my cabin. You're welcome to have this.'

Maureen was touched. 'It's very kind of you to offer, and thank you for your concern,' she squinted at his name badge, 'Tad, but it's not asthma. I was practising a special yoga breathing technique.'

'R—ight.' He said slowly, and then it was his turn to squint intently. 'Hey, you know you look familiar. Have you sailed with us before?'

Maureen swiftly slid her glasses back into place and explained that she hadn't. She gave him the lowdown on being part of a band contracted for three months to the *Mayan Princess*.

'Kenny Rogers, you say. My folks are big fans, but I'm more a hip-hop man myself.'

The unmistakable sound of a glass breaking brought the conversation to a close as Tad hurried off to help clean it up before he had a blood bath on his hands.

After forgetting about the yoga breathing, Maureen picked up her book again and closed it minutes later. She'd read the first paragraph so many times she could stand up and recite it like a sonnet. Her mind had kept returning to the tournament, playing it out like a film on the television set. A terrible, bad film you knew you should change the channel on, but you couldn't stop watching even though it would give you nightmares.

Donal had made it through to the table tennis final to be pitted against Bat Woman, as Maureen had predicted at the start of the tournament. The woman might be getting on in years, but she had more fancy footwork than Michael Jackson in the 'Beat It' video; Patrick had loved emulating the moves, too, when he was younger. She'd wiped the floor with her opponents thanks to a mean side spin serve, hoisting her slacks even higher, which hadn't seemed possible but clearly was, between games and in the end that serve had taken Donal out too.

Unfortunately, Maureen wasn't there to witness the last five minutes of the final, having been manhandled away from the tournament area by Christie's side-kick. It was the bubbling internal volcano's fault because as the match turned in the Bat Woman's favour, the thought of Donal not winning the *Mayan Princess* drink bottle prize had been too much for her and the volcano had erupted like Vesuvius. The words as she'd stood in the crowd watching the little woman do her worst had flown from her mouth in an unstoppable force.

'Smash her, Donal!' Swiftly followed by, 'Take her down!'

Not her finest moment.

The next thing Maureen knew, Christie was giving her a warning about inciting violence. She was marched off by a young woman in a similar uniform whose name she didn't catch but who did have a walkie-talkie. She was told to stay away from the tournament area. She hadn't; the stakes were too high and, waiting until the coast was clear, Maureen crept back to lurk in the fringes of the crowd, trying to see over the top of a sea of heads. Hearing the strident Eastend accent drifting through the gathered spectators, she immediately recognised it as belonging to the sinewy manchild.

'You know, Gina, it's not just you girls that get hit on by the passengers. I was in the lift earlier alone with that woman. The one who just got kicked out of the tournament a minute ago.'

'The mad Irish woman?' a female voice replied. 'What did she do?'

Maureen's ears and face were burning. *Yes what did I do?* She was rooted to the spot like a tree.

'Well, she made it obvious she was interested. She put on this "I've been smoking too many cigarettes" voice, think car driving over gravel, and started singing about how we've got tonight. I mean, it was clear what she was angling at.'

'OMG, that's terrible, Tony. And you were alone in the lift. Vulnerable.'

'I was vulnerable, yeah. The woman was a proper cougar.'

'We shouldn't have to put up with that sort of stuff. Sexual harassment isn't part of our contract. Are you going to report her?'

'No. But if it happens again, I will.'

Maureen wanted to shout, 'It won't happen again!' and simultaneously tap him on the shoulder and say she'd only sung the Kenny-Sheena hit to annoy him. He'd got the wrong end of the stick. But then she remembered she wasn't allowed to be here and, not wanting to create a bigger scene than she already had, Maureen decided it might be best to wait out the end of the match a safe distance away by the ship's railings. She'd get hold of yer man later and tell him it was a misunderstanding.

The sea breeze hadn't done much to cool her reddened cheeks, but it wasn't long before there was a round of applause, swiftly followed by a gasp from the crowd. What was going on? She didn't dare go back and check for herself and, craning her neck, she couldn't see a thing. A minute, maybe two passed and then Donal emerged flanked by John, Davey,

Niall and Carole. He was like a boxer being led through the crowd; he wasn't in those silky boxing shorts but he was in a comfortable blue pair of walk shorts with useful pockets that had flaps on either side. He wasn't clutching a *Mayan Princess* drink bottle either, and her heart sank at the realisation he'd lost. Donal McArthy was her man, though. Win or lose, as such, she'd stand by him. She waved out.

The party of five made their way over to Maureen.

'They're calling me the John McEnroe of the ping-pong world, Mo,' Donal said forlornly.

While Maureen asked what had happened, Niall and Carole peeled away to get drinks to lift their spirits.

'I held my own right to the end. I fought the good fight, Mo, but yer woman sent one too many side spin serves my way and took me out. I lost it.'

'He threw his paddle down so hard he snapped it,' Davey added.

'Oh, Donal, no. Not again.'

'I'm afraid so, Mo. I'm not proud of myself.'

'Tell her the rest,' John said, tearing his eyes away from a fella rolling a cigarette nearby.

'Yer Christie, Director of Entertainment and Table Tennis Tournament Referee, told me I'd caused wilful damage to cruise property. The replacement cost for a new paddle will be debited from our account.'

Davey piped up again, 'And, she said you're both banned from playing or being near the table tennis tables for life.'

'Tis true, and I'm sorry I behaved so badly, Mo. I don't know what came over me.'

'Me too, Donal. It's not in my nature to go around inciting violence, but—'

'Say no more, Mo. I think it's best we put the whole sorry saga behind us and never mention it again.'

'I think that's wise, Donal.' She didn't have it in her to confide the misunderstanding between herself and the sinewy manchild. The best thing they could do was lie low for the rest of the afternoon before their evening performance in the Havana Lounge.

'Do you mind if I join you, Maureen?'

Maureen, who'd been lost in thought there on her sun lounger, startled and then seeing it was Carole who was busy apologising for sneaking up on her, told her not to be silly and that she'd be most welcome to join her on one condition.

'And what would that be?' Carole asked.

'There's to be no mention of the table tennis tournament.'

'Deal!'

Chapter 14

♥

'Would you look at the state of those two?' Maureen shook her head. She'd discarded her hat and pushed her sunglasses on top of her head, having decided the risk of being recognised was low here in the shady nook of The Retreat. 'They're obviously making the most of their all-inclusive cruise package.'

Carole followed her gaze to where two bikini-clad women of middling years with drinks sloshing in their hands were dancing to the calypso beat emanating from the bar area, in heels no less. 'I wish my hips would let me break out moves like that, but I can't remember the last time I wore heels. My guess is they're newly divorced and celebrating their freedom with a cruise.'

The people-watching on a cruise should be added to the brochure at the travel agents as part of the onboard entertainment, Maureen thought, scanning the deck of The Retreat. The passengers were a colourful lot and Carole proved to be a tonic, enthusiastically joining the sport. She'd fetched them both a lemonade, and they'd adjusted the rungs of their loungers so they were sitting rather than lying. Then they'd begun their game of giving those that caught their eye a fictional history. It was the perfect distraction from the shenanigans of earlier.

CHAPTER 14   93

Maureen moved on to a silvery-haired couple sitting near the bar, holding hands under the table. The woman had a sophisticated martini before her, and he was sipping something amber-coloured on ice. 'Long since retired lawyers or doctors, and tis something special they want to commemorate with this cruise. Their diamond wedding anniversary, perhaps?'

'Hmm.' Carole sized them up from behind her sunglasses. 'Aren't they sweet? I'd say childhood sweethearts who've lasted the distance, and I'll run with your diamond anniversary celebration theory.'

'I hope Donal and I will be holding hands under the table in years to come.'

'Oh, I've seen how you two are around each other. I think you will. You're a perfect match.'

'So long as we stay away from the competitive sports.' Maureen looked at Carole, whose eyes had crinkled, and the next thing they were crossing their legs on their loungers, crying with laughter.

Maureen was hiccupping by the time they'd finished, and when she'd knocked back her glass of fizzy to see them off, she said, 'Of course, it's the second time round for us.' Carole, whom she'd initially thought hard work was proving to be easy company, and Maureen told the story of how she and Donal had met at just the right time in both their lives, confiding they'd given one another a new lease on life. She felt comfortable enough with the Australian woman now to dig a little deeper into her romantic background, telling herself it was purely for Niall's benefit. 'And yourself, Carole, is there, or was there, someone special in your life?'

'Once. I was married and thought Rob was the love of my life, but he announced he was no longer in love with me when I turned forty. You're going back fifteen years now and, with hindsight, I can see he did me a favour.'

'Still and all, what an eejit.'

'Eejit?'

'A fool, idiot – take your pick. My daughters would call him an "arse".'

'I'll take all three! Rob had a rather clichéd mid-life crisis. He went out and found the younger girlfriend, bought the flashy car and began dressing like he was twenty again. A balding twenty-something, might I add.' Her eyes twinkled, and Maureen sniggered at the picture she'd painted. 'It was all a bit tawdry and sad, to be honest, and at the time I certainly wasn't laughing about it, and neither was our daughter. Emma didn't take it well, understandably. She'd idolised her dad as girls often do.'

'They do; my girls thought the world of Brian, and rightly so. They found it hard when Donal came along, but he won them over.'

'I don't know him, obviously Maureen, but from what I've seen, he seems a lovely man.'

'Apart from when he gets a table tennis bat in his hand.' Maureen couldn't tell whether Carole had registered her remark. If she had this time she didn't crack a smile. A sadness had settled over her, which was evident in the slump of her shoulders. Maureen didn't know if it was down to talking about her ex-husband or mentioning her daughter, so she waited for her to speak.

'I have to say one of the hardest things I've ever had to do was keep my thoughts to myself regarding Emma's father. All I wanted to do was rant on about, about—'

'About what an eejit he was?'

'Exactly, but I knew that would make things worse for her. I never once bad-mouthed Rob to her. Well, not out loud anyway.' She side-eyed Maureen, who smiled.

'Well, then, you deserve a medal. Did this Rob ever see the error of his ways, or is he still trying to relive his youth?'

'He realised he'd made a mistake six months down the line, and I took him back mostly for Emma's sake but it wasn't the same. I was living a lie, and I woke up one day realising I no longer loved him. Respect and trust are vital ingredients in a marriage, and I'd lost both where he was concerned. I didn't have the energy or desire to let him try to regain either, not even for Emma's happiness, and we divorced.' Her sigh was almost a low whistle. 'I don't think she ever forgave me for that.'

Maureen wanted to say that that was hardly fair on her daughter's part, but then she knew motherhood could be a lopsided affair. Instead, she asked, 'And have you tested the romantic waters since?'

Carole shrugged. 'I put all my energies into Emma and then, when she left home, I went on a few dates mostly because my friends pestered me to, but nobody clicked. I don't know. It's probably down to me. Trust issues.'

'So, no Captain and Tenille fans in the dating pool until now?'

'You wouldn't be trying to matchmake Niall and I, would you, Maureen?' Carole raised her glasses, scrutinising Maureen. The twitch of her lips suggested she knew this was exactly what Maureen was up to.

'*Moi?*' Maureen feigned innocence, and Carole laughed. 'But if I was, I'd tell you that Niall is one of the most trustworthy fellas you'll ever meet. He'd hand it into the garda if he found a tenner in the street.'

'Garda?'

'Police.'

'Ah, I see.' Carole paused, plucking at the stripy towel and gazing at the pool before saying, 'I do like him, as it happens, and I think he likes me. Sometimes you click with someone from the get-go.'

'The Captain and Tenille.'

'The Captain and Tenille.' Carole grinned then turned to Maureen, her expression becoming serious. 'I've only just met him, Maureen, and this conversation is strictly between us.'

Maureen mimed sealing her lips. Then unsealed them to ask, 'Do you find him attractive though? It's important you know the physical attraction. I was always a Daniel Day-Lewis type of woman myself. You know, the chiselled jaw, Irish eyes and dark hair.' *And loincloth*, she thought, *mostly the loincloth*, but decided to keep that to herself. 'But when I met Donal, I realised it had been Kenny all along.'

'Well, Niall looks like an older, craggier, thinner Richard Gere. And I swoon every time I watch *An Officer and a Gentleman*.'

Maureen couldn't see it personally. She'd have said he was more Michael Wotsit from Monty Python but there you go, she wasn't about to rain on Carole's parade. So be it if she saw Richard Gere when she looked at Niall. Beauty was in the eye of the beholder and all that.

'Well, we're all on this ship together for three months, so that's plenty of time to see where it might take you and Niall.' Maureen shook her head, her dark hair bobbing about her shoulders as she lamented, 'An open mind is all that's needed in life, I always think, Carole. It would never have entered my head a few years ago that I'd be madly in love with a Kenny Rogers lookalike, singing the Sheena and Dolly parts with him and a tribute band on a Mexican Riviera cruise. Let alone getting paid to do so. Life is an adventure if you let it be.'

'That's true, but it's not always a good adventure,' Carole said softly.

'No. But we must journey through the bad bits to get to the good stuff.'

Carole nodded agreement, and they lapsed into a companionable silence until Maureen spied a woman around her age sitting companionably alongside a visibly pregnant younger woman. 'Now, look it over there. Those two are far too alike not to be mother and daughter. My guess is they've booked themselves on the cruise to enjoy some quality time together before the baby arrives. I'd say it's her first because look at what she's reading.' Maureen squinted, unable to read the title, but there was the unmistakable image of a baby on the cover. Then she swivelled to Carole, eager to hear her take on the scenario a few loungers away. She was alarmed to see her lips trembling and her chin wobbling and suspected tears would be glistening behind her sunglasses. 'Carole, are you all right?' It was a silly question, given she clearly wasn't.

'Not really, Maureen.' Carole sniffed.

'Don't move.'

Maureen hauled herself off the lounger and slipped her flip-flops on before heading to the bar where she grabbed a handful of paper serviettes, passing them to Carole on her return. Then she sat down, perching on the side of her lounger to face the other woman.

Carole accepted the serviette with a watery smile, lifted her sunglasses, and dabbed her eyes before giving her nose a good blow. She shot Maureen a grateful glance as she balled up the serviette and dropped it inside her empty glass. 'I wish Emma and I were like that.'

'Relationships between mams and daughters come in all shapes and sizes,' Maureen said gently. But Carole didn't seem to hear.

'We used to be close. When she was little, Emma was glued to my side. I had to coax her to join in things. It seems such a long time ago now. We haven't spoken in a year.' Carole's eyes welled up once more.

Maureen laid a hand on her forearm. 'I'm sorry to hear that.'

'It's mostly my fault.'

'Don't be so quick to blame yourself, Carole. As the mammy of three girls, I know daughters can be very quick to point their fingers at the mammy when things go wrong. Sure, Aisling's forever telling me she's always hungry because I used to hide the best biscuits so she wouldn't get her mitts on them.' Nothing sprang immediately to mind where Moira and Roisin were concerned. Still, she knew something would come to her, probably at 3am, the way the name of the actor in a particular movie you couldn't remember all evening would.

'The thing is, Maureen. Emma's right: it is my fault.'

The people and noise around them faded as Carole told Maureen her story.

Chapter 15

♥

Carole

The Circular Quay restaurant, with its fabulous water view, was not Carole's usual haunt. She thought that a Friday night takeaway in front of the tele with a glass of wine after a busy week's work was more her thing, her gaze straying to the harbour. The brilliant blue water was dotted with white sails as yachts breezed about and ferries plied their trade. Tonight, however, she felt sure it was a celebratory occasion that deserved to be noted even if the 'fine dining' tag on the popular restaurant seemed to be a licence to dish up minuscule, albeit artily presented, portions.

She switched her gaze back to her plate, eyeing the single scallop basking in a puddle of green sauce with an orange edible flower floating alongside it, and thought that, at this rate, she might have to call through the McDonald's drive-thru for a burger on the way home. Emma's plate was empty, she saw. The lamb cutlet must have been delicious. For a moment, she was tempted to pick up the bone and chew on it, get her money's worth. The thought of the look of horror on the wait staff silently gliding between tables were she to do so made her smile.

To be fair, Carole couldn't fault the atmosphere or service and it was special to be seated across from her beautiful daughter, whom she didn't get to catch up with as much as she'd have liked to since Emma had met Carlos. They were both so busy with work. Emma was all over the show with the music therapy classes she offered and private piano tuition, which paid the bills in the expensive city where they lived. She was also contracted on exciting occasions by the Sydney Symphony Orchestra.

'A chip off the old block' was how she'd heard her only child described more than once. Still, while Carole had had to work hard at her musical talent, she believed Emma was a gifted pianist. Her daughter had that special something that would see her soar in the classical world if she followed the right path, which was why when she'd heard about the repetiteur pianist opening at the New York Metropolitan Opera through her contacts Carole had been quick to push Emma to begin the lengthy application and audition process. It was a role that would see her accompanying singers and instrumentalists during rehearsals and much more. Most of all, though, the prestigious and coveted position would open doors for her in classical music. Carole's breath caught in her throat just thinking about it, and today was the day Emma heard back about whether she'd been successful.

Carole had booked this evening, having decided she'd order bubbles whether or not her daughter would be winging her way to the Big Apple. She didn't want Emma to feel like a failure; the fact that she'd gone so far with the application process was something to celebrate as far as she was concerned. However, Carole didn't doubt for a moment she'd not been offered the position.

The glow from the setting sun streaming through the floor-to-ceiling windows had turned her daughter's skin golden and even though she knew pride came before a fall it still swelled in Carole. She set her knife and fork down, dimly aware Emma was gushing about a film she'd seen with Carlos the other night. Goodness knew Carole had not achieved much in this life but when she looked at her daughter, her greatest accomplishment, that no longer mattered.

Emma was so relaxed and at home in the upmarket eatery's minimalist surroundings amongst Sydney's well-heeled – unlike herself. Carole felt like she should be whispering, and on her best behaviour: a child playing dress up in her new dress. Her toes were pinching in high heels she was unaccustomed to wearing, too, and she knew she'd thanked the waiter a little too effusively as he saw them to their table. However, her daughter had a natural confidence that allowed her to easily slot into any social situation. It was a trait she certainly hadn't inherited from her mother. To be fair to herself, Carole hadn't been schooled privately and given all the advantages she'd ensured Emma had. Some of that self-assurance was inherited, too. It came from Rob, her ex, who'd always been very sure of himself and his path in life, or at least he had been until his mid-life aberration.

Guilt twinged at not having invited him to join them tonight, knowing she'd been selfish, but she saw so little of Emma these days and when they did manage to catch up Carlos was always with her. She'd stressed it was a mother-and-daughter evening when inviting Emma to dinner.

Looking at her now, her golden daughter was sipping her – what was it she was drinking? Elderberry something – Carole's heart was fit to burst. They hadn't had an easy road, especially after the divorce which Emma, unfairly to her mind, had blamed her for. Rob had been the one who'd gone off the rails and cheated, not Carole. She'd done her best to forgive and forget but she didn't have it in her and, in the end, she'd asked him to move out permanently. There were times Carole wondered if she'd done the right thing, throwing herself into work the way she had after the divorce, but it had been her refuge and a necessity.

The Surrey Hills private girls school where she taught had discounted Emma's annual fees, which Rob had contributed to. Still, so many other things went hand in hand with that sort of exclusive education. The rowing Emma enjoyed as a respite from music, the class trips to Europe, and the cost in general of keeping up with her peers whose parents moved in a financial league Carole and Rob did not. She slogged away at the private piano lessons of an evening and Saturday mornings that paid for all those extras designed to produce a well-rounded, confident young woman who would leave school with the world at her fingertips.

Was it worth it? Carole wondered, sitting back in her chair and taking a pensive sip of wine. Absolutely. And suppose Emma announced she was off to New York to take up the opportunity of a lifetime? In that case, she'd gladly do it all over again. She'd do it all again either way.

'Eat your scallop, Mum, before it goes cold.'

Carole, who'd only been half-listening to her daughter's chatter, returned to the present with a surge of impatience. Why did she feel like Emma was skirting around the edge of what she knew her mother was desperately waiting to hear? Nevertheless, she dutifully popped the shellfish in her mouth, barely tasting it but making the requisite 'Mmm, lovely' noises. She swallowed, 'So, come on, Em, stop teasing. Were you offered the role or not?'

Emma's eyes flitted about the full restaurant before returning to meet her mother's expectant gaze.

'Yes. I was offered the contract.'

'Oh!' Carole had been expecting this reply but still she clapped her hands, causing several heads to turn. She didn't care and wasn't sure whether she would laugh with the excitement or cry!

'Mum, calm down.' There was a mix of irritation and hesitancy in Emma's tone that if she'd not been so overwhelmed by the news Carole might have picked up on; as it was she barely heard her.

The muted conversations and chink of cutlery resumed around them once more as Carole steepled her hands to her mouth as if in prayer. 'Congratulations, sweetheart. I always told you that hard work gets rewarded. You deserve this.' She was definitely going to cry; the lump was forming in her throat, and her eyes were beginning to smart. 'Do you remember when you'd moan about me making you practice when your friends were going to the beach? Well, where are those friends now? Look where you'll be going! New York, Emma. The Big Apple. We've got to celebrate with champers.' She went to raise her hand to get the wait staff's attention but Emma pushed it down swiftly with her own.

'When you've finished patting yourself on the back, Mum, I want you to listen to what I've got to say.'

Carole stopped short, staring across the table, thinking she'd misheard what Emma had just said to her, but a set to her daughter's jaw told her otherwise. Why was she going off script and looking angry instead of elated? Uncertainty saw Carole begin babbling. 'You don't like bubbles? Who doesn't like bubbles?' Then dislodging her hand from beneath Emma's she fanned herself with it. 'It's hot in here, don't you think?'

'Mum, would you stop it and just listen to me for once in your life.'

But Carole didn't want to hear what she had to say and if she kept talking herself she wouldn't have to listen to what her motherly sixth sense already knew was coming. So, scooping up a little of the green sauce congealing on her plate, she tasted it before holding the spoon out for Emma to try. 'It's very punchy.'

Emma batted her hand away and the spoon clattered to the table, leaving a green stain.

Carole stared at it, and she began to feel sick.

'Sorry. I didn't mean to do that, Mum, but you never listen to me.' Emma's voice had gone up a notch and sounded like a petulant teenager.

'I do.' Carole raised her gaze to see Emma shake her head.

'No, Mum. You don't because if you did you'd have heard me trying to tell you repeatedly that music therapy is my passion. I want to do that and share my life with Carlos here in Sydney. I don't want to live your dreams.'

Now Carole was shaking her head, on the defence. 'I thought it was your dream. And why apply, go through all that wasting everybody's time, including your own, if it's not what you wanted? I don't understand, Emma.'

Emma's eyes were sparking. 'You told me so many times that it was what I wanted, what I'd been working for my whole life, and I believed you.'

Had she? Yes, she supposed she had, but wasn't it true? Why else had Emma practised so hard? She hadn't forced her to sit at that piano. Emma wanted to. Hadn't she? Carole studied her daughter's face, hoping to see the answers, but she didn't recognise this young woman pointing the finger of blame her way. Deja vu replaced confusion. They'd been here before. Oh, not here in the restaurant per se, but in this situation, Emma shouting that the divorce, her dad cheating, and coming back only to leave because she, Carole, was making him go was all her mum's fault. While the theme was different, the story was the same. Anger crackled, flared and then died, her voice cracking as she said, 'I've given you everything, Emma. It's all been for you, and it's still not enough.'

As Emma's voice rose, people's heads tilted toward their table: listening to the unfolding drama. 'And don't I know it, Mum. It's all I've heard my whole life. How hard you've worked so I can have the opportunities you never had. Well, guess what? I didn't want to attend a stuffy private school where I didn't fit in. I didn't want to go on expensive overseas class trips or spend every spare hour practising piano. And when I tried to tell you that, you didn't listen.'

'Oh, play it again, Sam,' Carole shot back.

'It's true, you don't. You never listen, and it was easier to go along with it all, with everything, even applying for the repetiteur position at the fricking Metropolitan Opera, for God's sake!'

Carole flinched as if she'd been slapped, and as the oxygen fuelling Emma's fury ran out, she sat back in her seat. But if Carole thought she was spent, she was wrong. There was more to come.

'You did do me a favour in a round-about way. When the email said the position was mine, I knew I should feel elated but I didn't. It helped crystalise what I want, and that's to branch out into my own musical therapy practice and be with Carlos. But most of all, I want to be the best Mum I can be to our baby. You're going to be a granny, Mum.'

Carole felt like she'd stepped into an abyss and was freefalling. She grasped hold of the table, needing to feel something solid beneath her fingertips. 'What did you say?'

'You're going to be a grandmother. I'm three and a half months' pregnant.' Emma's face was hopeful as she looked at her mother.

Carole knew this was her chance to put things right between them. All she had to say was, 'That's wonderful, sweetheart.' Or, 'I'm so happy. So excited for you and Carlos.' Something along those lines, only she couldn't. All she could think about was how Emma had more talent in her little finger than she had despite her years of practising, wanting, and needing to be the best. Now, she was throwing it all away, and it was all down to her having met Carlos. And so, instead of reaching for her daughter and sweeping away their angry exchange with a hug, she stood up and pushed her chair back. 'You stupid, stupid girl. You'll regret this one day when you realise you were too young to get married, especially not to the first man who came along. And you're far too young to be a mother.'

Emma was pale and she opened her mouth, but Carole wasn't going to let her get a word in. She'd said more than enough for one night. 'One day, when you're knee-deep in dirty nappies, you'll wake up and think about everything you could have done with your life. I only hope, Emma, that your child doesn't turn around in years to come, pointing the finger at you and saying everything is your fault. I'll fix up the bill on my way out.'

The blood was rushing in Carole's ears as she walked away, her heart beating hard. She wouldn't look back, she resolved, and she didn't.

Chapter 16

Carole finished her story and Maureen was ready with another serviette, which she took gratefully. She was tearful and exhausted, yet at the same time it was a relief to have offloaded the great weight of her estrangement from Emma and her grandchild onto someone neutral's shoulders. It wouldn't change anything but a problem shared and all that. When she'd finished wiping her eyes and blowing her nose, she was taken aback to see Maureen holding her arms out, beckoning her in for a hug.

'We don't know one another well, Carole, but I have a feeling we'll be firm friends by the time our cruise contracts are up, and I think we know one another well enough now for a hug. Don't you?'

Carole hesitated. She wasn't usually an overly tactile person. Still, she'd just shared her very personal story with this little woman from Ireland, whom she'd had reservations about initially. They were opposites because her nature was naturally reserved, whereas Maureen was gregarious and, perhaps, a little bossy. Despite this, she'd warmed to her. Carole was also self-aware enough to understand her standoffishness had kicked in as a defence mechanism to ward people off after the apocalyptic dinner with Emma. This was down to shame. How could she tell people she'd fallen out with her own child so spectacularly? So she'd kept her distance, not even telling her smattering of close friends; they'd only tell her how foolish she'd been. That was something she'd already worked out. However, Maureen persevered by pushing through the wall she'd erected around herself. Carole suspected she'd smiled more in the short time she'd been on board the *Mayan Princess* than the entire last twelve months.

There was no judgment in Maureen's brown eyes, only concern, and suddenly a hug felt like the best offer she'd had all day. So, breaking character, Carole leaned in to draw comfort from the human connection. The weepiness returned as she felt Maureen pat her back and, sniffing, she mumbled, 'I didn't mean the awful things I said to Emma.'

'Of course you didn't.'

It had been so long since someone had held her and comforted her like her mum used to when she was a child, but Carole knew she didn't deserve Maureen's sympathy. She pulled away from the embrace, searching for another serviette. 'Actually, that's not true. I did at the time. I meant every single awful word of it. If it hadn't been for Carlos coming on the scene, she'd have stayed on course. I couldn't believe she was throwing away the opportunity of a lifetime, everything she'd worked so hard for. I mean, a baby? Why *then*? If she was serious about Carlos, why not in ten years when her career was established? And if he was serious about her, he should have been supporting her career, not derailing it.'

'Oh, Carole.' Maureen was reminded of all her emotions when she'd learned Moira, who'd had a complicated time of things, was pregnant.

'No,' Carole held her hand up, 'let me finish, Maureen. I refused to see the value in Emma's music therapy work or how rewarding she found it. I decided it was a stopgap until doors began opening for her. Then, as the weeks ticked by, I realised that New York, the Metropolitan Opera, was never Emma's opportunity of a lifetime. It was mine. Emma had already found her niche, her passion. Everything else, all those auditions, was for my benefit. It took me a good month or so to calm down and see things clearly but, when the blinkers fell off, I understood I'd pushed my dreams onto her. Not once did I stop to consider she might not want the same things I once had. Poor Emma didn't know how to get that through to me.'

Maureen took Carole's hands in hers then. 'Listen to me now.'

She was what Carole's mum would call a proper bossy boots but she also had a knack for making you do what you were told, so Carole decided to do exactly that and listen.

'You're not alone there. We're none of us perfect mams, but if we're a good mammy then we do what we think is best for our children and, sure, wasn't that what you thought you were doing?'

Carole's watery gaze settled on Maureen, and she felt the older woman squeeze her hands as she nodded. Did Maureen have a point? Was it time to stop with the self-flagellation? She had done what she'd thought was best, and not once had it occurred to her that might be wrong for her child. Wasn't her insistence on not wasting her talent what had led Emma to a job she loved?

'We all want our children to achieve more than we did. It's human nature, and I know first-hand how hard it is to accept they're no longer branches of ourselves but their own people who'll go down paths we might not choose.'

Maureen was a very sensible woman, Carole thought.

'What it comes down to, Carole, is this. Is she happy, your Emma?'

'I think so. I haven't seen her since I walked out of the restaurant but Rob's told me she and Carlos are a good match and that motherhood suits her. She had a little girl four months ago, Charlotte; she's the dearest little baby with wisps of dark hair, just like her mum had when she was born.'

Carole's gaze dropped, her voice barely louder than a whisper. 'I've only seen her in the photographs Rob sent me.'

'I can see how badly you're hurting.'

'There's a hole in my heart, Maureen. I'd give anything to hold Charlotte in my arms and to hug my Emma again.'

'Anything meaning accept her chosen route, and Carlos?'

Carole's nod was emphatic.

'Have you tried to tell Emma how you feel?'

'So many times. I've telephoned but she won't talk to me, and I called around to hers and Carlos's flat but she didn't want to see me. I've written letters and emailed them, but I don't think she reads them. Rob's tried talking to her for me, too, but she doesn't want to hear what I've got to say.' Carole's answer to this radio silence from her daughter was to put as much distance between them as she could. It was simply too painful to know she was near and yet so far. One of her student's mothers put the idea in her head of applying for work on the cruise ships when she raved about a recent holiday. So, she'd done just that and had been offered the gig on board the *Mayan Princess*. She'd thrown caution to the wind, jacked in her job and given her private tuition pupils the heave-ho telling anyone interested that a sea change was good for the soul. Besides, the opportunity to be paid to travel was too good not to take up. The truth was the Mexican Riviera was a satisfactory distance from Sydney and on a cruise she didn't always have one ear out for the phone, hoping it would ring or praying that there'd be a knock on the door. At sea, she was uncontactable until the ship docked at her scheduled ports. Then, the ball was in her court because it was up to her whether she checked her email.

Carole had convinced herself the pain of being estranged from her only child, from not even having seen her first grandchild, would hurt less if she put distance between herself and the wound. Now, it would seem no amount of distance would make the pain go away. She told Maureen all of this, adding, 'I had to give up in the end.'

'No, no, no. That won't do, Carole. We don't ever give up on our children. Emma's hurt, is what she is, and that baby girl needs her nana. And do you know what else?'

'What?'

'If you open your heart to Carlos and stop seeing him as the enemy, you might gain a son and get your daughter back.'

Carole had never thought about it like that. A son as well as a daughter. 'I'd like that, but I've told you I've tried and tried to reach out. It's impossible if she won't listen to what I want to say to her.'

They lapsed into thoughtful silence.

'The pair of you need your heads banging together,' Maureen muttered, frowning, and if Carole had known her a little better then she'd realise that frown meant she was plotting.

'You've certainly got a way with words, Maureen.'

But Maureen didn't reply. She was tapping her index finger on her chin. 'Hmm, I wonder,' she said half to herself.

'Wonder what?'

Maureen's gaze came back into focus. 'I wondered if you've ever tried speaking to Carlos.'

'No. I'd be the last person he'd want to talk to.'

'Well, that's your answer then.'

'You've lost me.'

'Emma won't hear you out, but I bet she'd listen to Carlos.'

'Maureen, what are you getting at?'

'Tomorrow, when we're in port, you should contact him.'

Carole looked aghast at the idea and quickly said, 'I don't have his number. I don't even have an email address for him.'

'Then reach out to your ex and ask him to send it to you. The only way to put things right is to ring Carlos and tell him everything you've told me about how sorry you are for what you said.'

'It is?'

'It is.'

Yes, Carole thought, *she was right. I am sorry from the bottom of my heart.* Maureen definitely had a bossy streak, but she'd do as she suggested because she had nothing more to lose and everything to gain.

Chapter 17

♥

Maureen stuffed her book into her bag, ensuring her hat and sunglasses were firmly in place before leaving The Retreat. She wanted to venture back to the cabin and check on Donal to see if he'd nodded off. He was no good when he napped too long in the afternoon. She owed it to the country music fans aboard the *Mayan Princess* to ensure they weren't graced with a groggy and, yes, grumpy Kenny for The Gamblers' gig later. Carole, however, had opted to stay a little longer, spent from all she'd shared, stretching out on her lounger and closing her eyes.

It had been tempting to swing by the Lido Buffet for a late afternoon tea graze, but Maureen decided an early dinner was a smarter idea. She didn't like performing on a full stomach in case she got the indigestion. It was very hard to keep the rhythm with the tambourine and suck on the Rennies at the same time. Nobody would say, 'Well done, sweetheart,' like she did the twins if she brought up wind during her Sheena or Dolly set.

With all the eating she'd done since discovering the wonderland that was the Lido Buffet, Maureen opted to take the stairs. As she reached the tenth-floor landing, the fleeting thought of whether or not Kenny occasionally took afternoon naps crossed her mind. He was bound to, was her consensus, as the unmistakable sound of a baby crying on the floor below distracted her. She hurried down the stairs to the ninth floor like a magnet pulled toward the fridge door. The piercing sound tugged at her, and a wave of pity over Carole's predicament washed over her too. To never have even seen your grandchild, well, it was unimaginable. Still and all, she had high hopes that her plan for her new friend to reach out to Carlos and mend bridges would soon have mother and daughter reunited. The thought of Carole's face when she saw her little grandbabby for the first time made her eyes smart. The homesickness that followed this as she thought of her own little ones took her by surprise. She'd only been away for a week, but this would be the longest stretch she'd ever been parted from any of them. Thank goodness they'd all be barrelling on board with their mammy and daddies in a month. That was when she stopped short in her tracks because without even realising she'd done so, she'd followed the wailing around the corner to the lift where a young mammy around Moira's age was jiggling a plump baby girl frantically trying to get her to stop crying. The poor girl was almost in tears herself. Maureen saw several passengers giving her and her crying child a wide berth, opting for the stairs instead.

People could be so intolerant, she thought. *Sure, they were all babies with wants and needs once.* 'What's her name?' Maureen asked over the wailing din.

'Laura.' The woman gave Maureen a frazzled smile. 'And I wish this lift would hurry up.'

'Oh, that's a lovely name, so it is. How old is she?'

'Thank you. Nearly ten months, and I blame her dad, who is right now picking up our toddler from Little Minnows, for booking a cruise with a baby and a two-year-old. "We'll make memories," he said. "It will be a chance to relax as a family." Well, look how that's going.' She glanced about self-consciously.

'Is Laura hungry?'

'No.'

'Tired?'

'Yeah, a little. She's going to be a nightmare to put down for a nap, though.'

'In need of changing?'

She patted her daughter's nappy-clad bottom. 'No.'

'Right then.' Maureen rolled up the sleeves of her caftan. She'd have to improvise and do the Kenny bits and Dolly's, but it wouldn't be the first time that the 'Islands in the Stream' song crooned solely from her lips. Little Laura turned toward her as she reached the Dolly part, the tension seeping out of her, and her face unscrewed until she laid her head on her mother's shoulder contentedly.

'Oh my goodness, you're like the baby whisperer.'

Maureen beamed. 'It works a treat for my granddaughter.'

'Can I hire you? Like on an as-and-when-needed basis?'

Maureen wasn't sure if her leg was being pulled but was spared from answering by the ding of the lift. 'Off you go now. You'll find she'll go out like a light and be altogether different when she wakes.' She said ta-ta to the sleepy Laura and gave her mother a reassuring smile that said, 'You've got this,' before they disappeared from view inside the lift. She was about to continue on her merry way when she spotted a sinewy shadow and spun around to see it was him, Tony, the manchild who thought she was on the prowl for a toy boy. Wumph: heat raced up her neck and into her face. 'Yoo-hoo,' she trilled, charging toward him, determined to put him straight. She'd tell him in no uncertain terms that Maureen O'Mara had a man friend and was not a cougar!

Tony glanced over his shoulder at the noise. For a moment, his resemblance to a meercat surveying the African savannah was stunning. Then, as Maureen advanced toward him, he sprang into life and began charging through the people, making their way down the corridor as though she were a hit woman and him her target. It was like a scene from a James

Bond film with Maureen, the femme fatale assassin, in her flapping caftan as she gave chase.

'Hey Bob, isn't that the woman who got escorted away from the table tennis tables earlier?'

Now, it was Maureen who froze in her tracks. It was too late but she pulled her hat down as low as it would go, only to find her vision impaired as she skulked away. Tripping over would only draw further attention to herself, and she decided the best thing to do was take it off altogether as she all but fled to the stairs.

***

Maureen banged the cabin door shut, leaning against it to catch her breath. She closed her eyes briefly. She'd made it back without anyone else pointing her out. Tony, the man-child, would have to wait for another day.

Donal was wide awake and watching the credits roll on a film. 'Are you alright there, Mo? You're looking very flushed, so you are. Did you decide to visit the gym?'

'No. I ran down the stairs all the way from the ninth floor. You won't believe the afternoon I've had, Donal.'

Donal patted the space beside him on the bed. 'Come and tell me all about it.'

Maureen pushed off from the door and kicked off her flip-flops, padding toward the bed.

'You've just missed your favourite film.'

'Ah no, Donal, don't tell me.'

'Alright. I won't.'

Maureen flopped down next to him. 'It wasn't—'

'It was Mo. *The Last of the Mohicans*.'

'No!'

'I shouldn't have told you. Now then, what have I missed?'

Maureen told him she'd spent a pleasant few hours getting to know Carole and left it at that.

'I'm forgiven for my unsportsmanlike behaviour then?'

'There's nothing to forgive, and I was hardly a model citizen myself.'

'You could say you were put under "citizen's arrest" by your Director of Entertainment's sidekick though.' Donal made the inverted commas with his fingers and began chortling away, making the bed shake. Maureen failed to see the humour in having been manhandled away from the table tennis tables, so she decided it was time to move things along, telling him about her impromptu baby whisperer performance.

'It's a good job the toddler Kiera wasn't here to see it, Donal. She might have got upset seeing her nana singing to another babby like so. A wee dote she was, too.' Kiera had a territorial streak in her, just like her mammy.

'I think you'd be right there, Mo.'

'Donal, there's something else.' Maureen hesitated, unsure she could bring herself to share the label she'd been pegged with by a fellow *Mayan Princess* entertainer.

Donal, sensitive as ever to the subtle nuances in Maureen's voice, picked up on this. 'I'm all ears.'

'It's just, well, it's just that it's mortifying, so it is.'

'You know you can tell me anything.'

That was true enough, and Maureen haltingly explained the misunderstanding between herself and the manchild, then thumped Donal on the back. His chortle had morphed into a cough. 'That will teach you for laughing, Donal McCarthy. You want to have seen him just now. He tossed his head like a wild pony when he saw me. Sure, I thought he'd whinny before stampeding off like so.' Her mouth began twitching at the imagery, and it wasn't long before they were roaring laughing together.

Maureen felt much improved, her equilibrium restored by the time she'd stopped with the hiccups all that laughing had brought on. It was good for the soul, the laughter, she thought, as her tummy gave a loud rumble.

'Is it time for a bite to eat, Mo?'

'An early dinner would be just the ticket.'

'Right so.' Donal sat up. 'We'll hold our heads up high out there, Mo. Brazen it out. People have short memories. They'll have forgotten all about the table tennis by tonight.'

'I'm sure you're right, Donal.'

Chapter 18

It was very hard to be self-disciplined with all the food offered at the Lido Buffet, Maureen and Donal agreed. Especially given that they were paying a reasonable price. This was why they'd all but rolled back to their cabin. They'd not seen the rest of The Gamblers, nor had Maureen glimpsed Carole. She hoped she'd managed to relax and rejuvenate herself for her evening's performance in the Atrium Lounge.

'I'm going to be setting the alarm for the Sunrise Yoga class tomorrow morning, Donal,' Maureen called out as he finished getting ready. There was no room for them to change in the space between the wardrobe and bathroom simultaneously, so Maureen suggested that Donal get ready first while she did her makeup. That way, he could head to the Havana Lounge and help set up with John, Davey and Niall. She wouldn't be far behind.

'Fair play to you, Mo. I think I might take a turn on the treadmill myself tomorrow.' There was a grunting sound.

'Are you alright there, Donal?'

'Just doing up my fly, Mo. I'm telling you now, I won't fit my Kenny suit in another week if I don't curtail my portion size and start doing some exercise.'

'We're going to have to be disciplined, Donal, or my silver lamé dress will hang next to your Kenny suit, not seeing the light of day for the remainder of our contract.'

'You're not wrong there, Mo. Now, will I do?' Donal emerged from the wardrobe alcove, transformed from the man in comfortable walk shorts with pockets who'd lost the plot with a ping-pong paddle into a handsome, big teddy bear-like country music icon.

'You'll do very nicely.' Maureen remembered the red-headed woman bothering him at the omelette station that morning and vowed to stand by her man this evening if she happened along to the Havana Lounge with any ideas. She got up from the chair in front of the dressing table mirror and fluffed about with his lapels. 'I'm a lucky woman, Donal McCarthy.'

'It's me who is lucky, Mo.'

They smiled at each other, and Maureen gave him a chaste kiss, not wanting to get lipstick all over him. Then, silently thanking Him upstairs for sending Donal her way, she shooed him out the door. She had things to do, starting with warming her voice up. The cabin didn't have the best acoustics but needs must and, clearing her throat, Maureen began to tra-la-la-la her way through the scales. Only once she was satisfied it would be a doddle to hit Sheena's high notes did she discard her dressing gown and unhook her silver lamé gown from the hangar.

The sucky-in knickers were a blessing, she thought, wriggling the dress's zipper into place and then slipping her feet into the sparkly heels that made her feel a million dollars; she gave herself a once-over in the mirror. 'You'll do nicely too, so you will, Maureen O'Mara.' She smiled at her reflection, pleased, and couldn't resist giving herself a 'come hither' look in the mirror. It was a look best left for the privacy of the cabin if she didn't want all and sundry to 'come hither' while she was banging her tambourine. With a fluff of her hair and a moment's mourning over the loss of her platinum wig, she picked up her bottle of Arpège. 'The finishing touch,' she said aloud, as you do on your own in a cruise cabin, and spritzed generously. Too generously.

Maureen was standing in a fragrant Arpège cloud, which would be all well and good if she had a window to open. The tickle at the back of her throat where the perfume was catching became a choking cough and she staggered out of the cabin, flapping the door back and forth to air it out as she wheezed and coughed.

'Maureen, did you have the fish curry too?' Tomasina asked in her accented English as she emerged from her cabin in a sparkling outfit. Only hers was barely there and had tassels.

'No. I did not.' Maureen croaked indignantly. 'I was heavy-handed with the perfume, is all, and I'm airing the room out so Donal and myself can breathe later.'

'Poor Pawel, he had the fish curry. I told him not to but these men,' Tomasina made a *pfft* sort of a noise, 'do they listen?'

Maureen would have liked to have said that her Donal was a very good listener but felt this would be an annoying response, so she opted to say nothing as Tomasina frowned, her nose wrinkling. 'Pawel, he is not good with the fish curry. I told him if he eats it again I might not return when he makes me disappear in our act.' She sniffed as she reached Maureen, who was still flapping the door. 'I can smell it now, your perfume. I like it. It is preferable to the fish curry.'

'I'm pleased to hear it,' Maureen muttered as the younger woman sniffed again.

'It has a vintage elegance and glamour, Maureen.' Then, taking in Maureen's silver lamé dress, she endeared herself to Maureen forever by adding, 'Like yourself.'

If not for the word 'vintage' Maureen would have adopted her as her long-lost Polish daughter on the spot. Deciding to disregard it and roll with 'elegance' and 'glamour', she thanked Tomasina. 'Why don't you stand inside our cabin for a few seconds? Get the smell of fish curry from your nostrils with the added bonus of smelling elegant and glamorous. Arpège is my signature perfume.'

Tomasina did just that, standing with her arms outstretched as though about to be spray-tanned as she told Maureen how much she liked her dress.

Maureen, whose arm was getting weary from all the door flapping, gave her a coy smile and said, 'Why, thank you,' in a Southern drawl which saw Tomasina frown once more.

'Why are you speaking in that even stranger accent than your Irish one, Maureen?'

Maureen thought about explaining why she pretended to be a Southern belle only to realise she didn't know the answer. Instead, she asked where Pawel was, hoping the fish curry wouldn't see him holed up in his cabin all night because, from what she'd seen of his and Tomasina's magic show, they were a double act.

'He's already backstage. I had to return to the cabin because I forgot my good luck charm. I never go on stage without it.'

Suppose Donal was attempting to saw her in half? In that case, she'd dare say she'd always have a good luck charm on her, too, Maureen thought, stepping aside as Tomasina exited the cabin. Checking she had her lanyard around her neck, she shut the door. 'Is it a rabbit's foot?' Maureen asked as they shimmered and shone their way toward the lift. She half expected to see a furry thing dangling off a key chain or clipped onto Tomasina's lanyard.

Tomasina side-eyed her. 'You are a funny woman, Maureen. Why would I carry a dead rabbit's foot? This is my good luck charm.' She dug into a minuscule hidden pocket on the hip of her costume to reveal a small brown pebble. 'In Poland, Amber is considered good luck. I find this with my brother on the coast.'

'Your brother who is in Ireland?'

As they stepped into the lift, pushing the buttons for their respective floors, Maureen took note of Tomasina's downcast expression, figuring this was down to her brother. 'And is he having the luck o' of the Irish with his brown pebble in Dublin?'

Tomasina shrugged. 'He says he is doing well in his emails but I know him, and I am sensing he's keeping something back from me and mama.'

'Hmm, like what, I wonder?'

'I don't know, but I am hoping he's not in some sort of trouble. He is my little brother. I worry.'

'Has he got himself in hot water before?'

'My brother is very clean, Maureen; he bathes daily!'

'No, Tomasina, I mean: has he been in trouble before?'

'Oh, then why would you not just ask this?' She shook her head. 'And no more so than any young man living away from home for the first time.'

The two women lapsed into silence and were pleasantly surprised to have a clear run in the lift. When Tomasina arrived at her floor she said goodnight to Maureen, who called after her, 'Break a leg, Tomasina!'

'Maureen, why would you say this terrible thing to me?' Tomasina held the lift open with her hand as her eyes flashed, demanding an explanation.

The language barrier was proving tricky, Maureen thought, all set to explain what the saying meant in the entertainment world in which they both moved.

Tomasina, however, had broken into a grin. 'I am pulling *your* leg. See, I too know some of these strange English sayings.'

Just then, the woman on the motorised scooter who'd attempted to ram-raid their full-to-capacity lift last night caught sight of Tomasina's tassels. She was so busy gawping that she veered off course, nearly taking out the pop-up perfume stand. Before Maureen could shout after her to keep her eyes on the road, so to speak, the doors closed. A second or two later she was sashaying down to the Havana Lounge, which was now magically transformed by haybales.

'How're you lads?' she greeted, joining the band where they were all fiddling with their equipment in the small area allocated for the band and dancing; even Donal was having a go. He had a microphone he was tapping on but no sound came from it. Maureen decided to throw caution to the wind and give him her 'come hither' look, gratified to receive a long, slow whistle in response from Donal. Unfortunately, the microphone chose that moment to screech into life as he whistled into it and several patrons nearby slapped their hands over their ears, wincing.

Donal apologised before breathing into the mic with a, 'Testing, testing, one, two, three.'

The lads told Maureen she looked very well in her silver lamé and, preening, she reached for her tambourine, which she'd charged Donal with looking after. She took her place to the side of Donal and checked out the audience, spotting a few ankle boots and Stetson hats in the mix.

'Ready?' Donal asked Maureen, Niall, Davey and John.

'Ready,' came the reply.

Donal leaned into the microphone again, tapping his foot. 'A one, a two, a one, two, three, four.'

They opened as they always did with the crowd-pleaser their band was named after, 'The Gambler', and it wasn't long before the dance floor was filled with Stetsons and ankle boots, all taking a turn.

Donal's whistle wasn't the only one Maureen received that night. The band finished their first half with 'Reuben James'. Donal announced a short break before stepping away from the stage area to order drinks, and mix and mingle their way around the Havana Lounge. Maureen was on a natural high as she always was during and after a show: relieved, too, that her voice hadn't let her down after her choking session earlier in the cabin. She'd been worried she'd be sounding more like Marianne Faithfull than Dolly, but the applause at the end of the song had said she'd nailed it. Sheena was for the second half, and the lads were talking about throwing in a Billy Ray Cyrus number to get the remaining slow pokes on the dance floor.

Niall was sidling out of the bar; she noticed, suspecting he was whipping out to watch Carole for five minutes. The lad was smitten! She was waiting at the bar to order a drink for herself and Donal, having left him chatting to an American couple who'd seen Kenny perform last year. Her gaze drifted around the lounge, pleased to note the red-headed omelette station woman had now taken a shine to Davey. At the same time, John captivated her friend with his drumstick-twirling prowess. Maureen mused that he was like one of those marching girls with their batons, recalling that Aisling had wanted to be a marching girl. It wasn't a match made in heaven, given she had a terrible rhythm. Maureen had suspected it was the white boots Aisling had coveted. She'd had a thing for shoes even back then. That was when Maureen saw him. He was breezing past the Havana Lounge with no cares in the world. Tony the Manchild.

There was no time to tell Donal she'd be back in a jiffy because her heels were already carrying her out of the bar as fast as her silver lamé gown would allow. This time, Maureen decided she'd use the element of surprise because she'd no doubt he'd run like the wind if she were to 'yoo-hoo' him again.

Her opportunity came as he paused to exchange flirty banter with the girl manning the pop-up jewellery stand. Maureen tip-toed up behind him and tapped him on the shoulder. 'Excuse me, young man. I'd like a word with you.'

Tony spun around, the colour draining from his face, his reaction so swift it left Maureen blinking in shock as he whipped out a silver whistle like the one a lifeguard at a pool would use and blew it hard. 'Back away from me.'

In shock at the unexpected shrill noise, Maureen nearly lost her footing, teetering on her heels as she did just that. Then, Tony shot off in a sinewy blaze of glory, leaving her and the girl flogging the gold bracelets and necklaces staring at one another open-mouthed.

Chapter 19

♥

Day 3 - Port of Call, Cabo San Lucas

It was a new day, Maureen thought, determined to cast Tony the Manchild and his self-defence whistle from her mind. Still, the memory of those curious onlookers – who upon hearing the shrill whistle blast had poked their heads around the Havana Lounge to see if an emergency lifeboat drill was happening – was mortifying. She'd herded them back inside the lounge before slinking to the bar to order the drinks she was supposed to be fetching. All she could hope for was that the magnificent champagne waterfall in the Atrium later that evening, as couples posed alongside it for professional photographs in their formal attire, had wiped the memory of the emergency lifeboat drill that never was from their minds.

Slipping into her Mo-pants, Maureen readied herself for a lovely zen sunrise yoga session on the Lido deck. She hoped it would restore her equilibrium because she'd not slept well. Her dreams had been peppered with court appearances where she was charged with being a cougar by a judge who was as sinewy as a chewy piece of chuck steak. Donal had already staggered off to the gym, still half-asleep, as he left the cabin in his least favourite pair of walk shorts with pockets, declaring them his workout shorts from hereon in. Maureen hoped Donal had listened when she called after him to warm up before leaping on the treadmill. Given that they'd be traipsing around Cabo San Lucas later this morning he'd need his sturdy walking legs. *Mind you,* she thought tucking her singlet top in, *it would serve him right if he did suffer.* She was still annoyed with his reaction to last night's mortifying pop-up-jewellery-stand incident. He'd roared with laughter when she came clean about what had happened with the Manchild.

If Donal thought she'd rub the Deep Heat on his legs later, like Moira and Aisling did Tom and Quinn when they stepped up their Dublin Marathon training, he had another thing coming. For one thing, she'd not packed a tube in their first aid kit, and the E45 cream would be next to useless although it might help clear up the dry patch on his knee. And, for another, she wasn't so inclined.

Maureen slipped her Bendy Yoga Ladies pink jacket off the hangar and put it on even though it was likely too hot to wear. Nobody could say she didn't support her daughters and their enterprises because she wanted to look the part and seize the opportunity to promote Roisin's Bendy Yoga Studio internationally.

Now, where were her flip-flops?

―――*ele*―――

The Lido deck was quiet, given the early hour, and the day was temperate and golden. She'd been right; it was too warm for a jacket, even at this early hour. For now, though, she'd keep it on until she'd given all the yoga devotees gathered for their sunrise session a good gawp at it. It was smart marketing because who knew? One of the passengers might be holidaying in Dublin in the future, feeling the need to stretch. They'd remember the woman in the snazzy pink jacket and its logo on the back advertising a Bendy Yoga Studio in Howth. The word would spread when whoever returned to their own country about the excellent yoga workout they'd had in Howth and then, before you knew it, Rosi would turn her Bendy Yoga Studio into a franchise and go global. All of which was thanks to this. She stroked the satiny fabric of the pink jacket.

Still and all, Maureen thought, unzipping it, she wasn't game to flash the jacket about Cabo San Lucas later because she guessed the day would have cranked into a scorcher by noon. A glance at her watch revealed five minutes until the 7am session began. She could see the mats were set out and slowly filling but she was eager to see if she could catch a glimpse of their first port of call even though they weren't due to arrive at the resort city until 11am. So she flip-flopped over to the ship's railing instead.

'Oh, would you look at that,' she breathed to the lone seagull perched on the rail, referencing the vista of glistening blue. Shading her eyes with her hands, she could see the haze of land in the distance. The view was more shimmery than her silver lamé gown, and she thought that was saying something.

Maureen's peripheral vision spotted movement and then she turned to see a woman in a fitted tank top and leggings hurrying past. Her heart sank. It was Christie, the Director of Entertainment. It would seem she was a woman of many talents. Pub quiz master, table tennis referee and yoga instructor. Maureen mooched over to the small gathering of women taking their places and stretching on the mats set out. Determined to get off on the right foot with Christie, she called out a good morning. 'Donal dedicated the "Daytime Friends" song to you last night, Christie, like he promised he would.'

Christie's eyes narrowed as she clocked who'd joined the session. 'You do realise yoga is non-competitive or combative, right?'

'I'm a regular on the Howth yoga circuit, Christie; my daughter has her own studio, so you don't need to tell me that.' Maureen spun round to give Christie a glimpse at the logo on the back of her jacket, then picked out a pink mat, subconsciously colour-coordinating. Remembering her stern word about warming up to Donal, she warmed up with a few lunges. They had the added benefit of ensuring everyone got a good look at her jacket, and sure enough . . .

'Honey, I love that jacket. It's so Rizzo from *Grease*. And where did you get those yoga pants? They look super comfortable.' A woman with a genuine Southern drawl around her age spoke up. She was sprawled on the mat next to Maureen's, plucking at her leggings. 'These are okay, aside from being able to see what you had for breakfast in them. And I had a plate that was all business for breakfast yesterday. I mean, I'm talking eggs, bacon, sausage, toast, and don't get me started on lunch and dinner.'

Maureen smiled. 'You're not alone there and thanks a million. These here,' she pulled at the fabric of her legwear, 'are Mo-pants.' She was about to tell the woman about her entrepreneurial yoga pant journey, swiftly following it up with a rundown on the Bendy Yoga Studio, when Christie eyeballed her and instructed them all to lie down comfortably. Maureen discarded her jacket, flapping it out to give anyone whose eyes were open one last look before taking up her position. She lay prone on the mat, feeling the rigid boards of the ship beneath her, and shut her own eyes.

Christie's voice was soothing as Maureen let the Director of Entertainment's words wash over her.

'Begin by taking a long, slow inhale past your ribs. Let your breath fill your belly, pushing it up.'

Maureen, peeking, noticed bellies popping up all over the show; it was a veritable mountain range of tummies.

'Exhale all the old air out and let the energising sea air work its magic.'

Maureen did so, but it wasn't sea air she could smell. Instead, the tempting aroma of sizzling rashers teased her. Her stomach rumbled audibly, and she apologised to the woman on her left and the man on her right, doing her best to concentrate on her breathing. It was no good; she wasn't getting into the flow of it because the bacon was very distracting and, she thought, her eyes narrowing as she side-eyed the man on her right, *there was always one.* Her toes curled as he began exhaling extra noisily through his nostrils. She thought the heavy breathers of the yoga world were so annoying. And yes, all right, Rosi had explained this was called Ujjayi breathing and was supposed to sound like a victorious ocean breath. Well, yer man there sounded more like a chronic sinusitis sufferer, and he wasn't very good at following instructions. Christie hadn't instructed them to do the Ujjayi breathing. He'd gone rogue on the breathwork.

At last, the class got properly underway with a series of stretches, which Maureen was familiar with, and soon progressed to a round of sun salutations. She was managing to tune Mr Heavy-breather out as they flowed into a proud warrior stance but, as she looked at her fellow warriors, she felt compelled to speak up. 'Excuse me, Christie,' she called to where Christie was in the side lunge pose with her arms outstretched, 'you've locked your back knee there, and so's everyone else. My daughter Rosi, you know, who owns a yoga studio. She's always quick to tell her students to soften their back knee when they're lunging. You don't want to strain your ligaments like so, and it stops you from engaging your other muscles.' Maureen was gratified to see a mass unlocking of back knees.

A variety of expressions flitted across Christie's face before she said through gritted teeth, 'Thank you, er—'

'Maureen O'Mara.' Maureen beamed over at Christie, sure she'd just ingratiated herself back into the Director of Entertainment's good books. 'From Ireland; Christie already knows

I'm here as part of the crew,' Maureen addressed the small group of keen yoga devotees. She told them she was the tambourinist and guest vocalist with The Gamblers, a Kenny Rogers tribute band, who played each evening in the Havana Lounge.

'Okay, moving right along into a pose I think some of us might find especially beneficial: humble warrior,' Christie instructed.

There was no call for Maureen to speak up again until she was standing on her right leg, her left leg crooked, and resting on her calf, her arms outstretched in tree pose. She tried channelling a majestic oak tree but felt she was more 'spindly poplar precariously swaying in a gale-force wind'. 'Excuse me, Christie,' she called over, 'Rosi likes to tell her pupils to imagine that their grounded foot is a tree root extending deep into the ground.' She wished she could do the soothing yoga voice, but it wasn't in her repertoire, as she added with another full wattage beam, 'It can be helpful.'

Feeling like the teacher's pet after class thanks to her handy tips, she bustled up to Christie. She told her about Rosi's impending holiday aboard the *Mayan Princess* and how she'd only be too happy to swap yoga notes with her.

Maureen was a little put out that instead of a grateful smile and, 'That would be wonderful, Maureen,' Christie looked as though she had overindulged on last night's fish curry. Oh well, she thought, there was no time for further chit-chat anyway: she and Donal were due to meet the lads and Carole in the Lido Buffet restaurant for breakfast at eight-thirty in readiness for their day in Cabo San Lucas. She'd need to go and shower for the exciting day of exploring that lay ahead.

Chapter 20

♥

Maureen and Donal were being jostled by excited passengers who'd also decided the best view of their arrival into Cabo, as she'd heard those in the know abbreviate the Mexican resort city's name to, was at the prow of the *Mayan Princess*.

'Look, there it is,' somebody shouted, and Maureen stood on tiptoes, craning her neck for her first glimpse of the Arch of Cabo San Lucas. 'Donal, it's just how the daily ship's newsletter described it. A mellow-hued rock, rising out of the sparkling Sea of Cortez: pass me the camera, quick!'

'Put the strap around your neck, Maureen, because I'll not be jumping in after it if you drop it. Who knows what's swimming about in that water.' Donal's gaze was wary as he passed the camera over, expecting to see a frenzy of great whites in the calm waters below, just waiting for a plump Irish cruise passenger to fall in. 'They've sharks in Mexican waters, you know. I saw them in Jacques Cousteau's documentary. Vicious they were, eating all the poor fish.'

Maureen thought it was good advice and draped the strap around her neck, taking aim with the camera just as the woman beside her knocked her, causing her to push the shutter. She thought the photo would be a blue blur, and her eyes narrowed as the woman didn't offer an apology. Two could play at that game. Then, recalling her determination to hang on to the lovely zen post-yoga feeling, Maureen elbowed Donal instead. 'It's gorgeous, isn't it?'

'You're not wrong there, Mo,' Donal said, rubbing his side. 'And go easy on me. My poor old muscles are seizing up. I didn't realise the rowing would be such a full-body workout.'

He'd told Maureen upon his sweaty return to their cabin earlier that the treadmills had all been in use so he'd hit the rowing machine, instead. She could tell from his red face he'd gone for gold and pretended he was trying out for the Irish rowing team. It was on the tip of her tongue to say, 'I told you so,' regarding the warm-up exercises or lack thereof. Still, she refrained because she was, after all, holding onto being zen.

The harbour ahead, where luxury yachts jostled alongside fishing boats, was small and, from what Maureen and Donal could see, packed with boats of all shapes and sizes. Donal's frown was deep as he pondered out loud the logistics of a ship the size of the *Mayan Princess* squeezing in amidst the fray.

'Don't worry, Donal. Captain Franco knows what he's doing.'

Donal began humming 'Stayin' Alive', and Maureen relayed a spot of trivia she'd gleaned from yesterday's pub quiz. 'Did you know you've the Bee Gees to thank for writing Kenny and Dolly the "Islands in the Stream" song?'

'They never.'

'They did. So think on, Donal McCarthy.'

The word 'tenders' was bandied about, and Maureen and Donal put two and two together. The ship would not be muscling its way into the harbour. Instead, they'd be boarding a tender boat to take them ashore. Deciding there was nothing more to see now, they edged away from the prow to search for Carole, Niall, John and Davey. The foursome wasn't hard to find seated around an open-air table near the pool with the remains of a late breakfast in front of them.

'We're making the most of the sun before it gets too hot to sit out in,' John informed them, drumming his fingers on the table, bouncing his knee and never taking his eyes off the man a few tables away who was close to eating the cigarette he'd smoked so far down. Maureen clicked her fingers in front of him, breaking the spell.

'Thanks, Mo. A weak moment, you know.'

Maureen slid his half-eaten toast under his nose. 'You're better off finishing this, John.'

Niall obligingly helped Donal find two extra chairs. At the same time, Davey chomped his way through the pastries he'd helped himself to, declaring them a grand way to finish breakfast. Carole meanwhile caught Maureen's eye and Maureen, taking the chair from Niall, slotted it in alongside her. 'All set for today?' The question was loaded because she hoped Carole wouldn't back down. Reaching out to her ex-husband for Carlos's contact details was the first step to putting things right with her daughter.

'All set.' Carole sounded confident and reassured Maureen, so much so that she thought how well she'd slotted into their group. She was pleased to have made a new friend as she tuned in to the story she was telling them. It was about a couple who requested Carole play 'Lady in Red' during her set last night because it was their song. Only the woman stalked off halfway through Carole's piano keyboard version because her husband was eyeing a tall blonde who happened to be in red. Listening, Maureen was glad she'd not let her first impressions of Carole put her off because she was lively and good fun once you got past her ice queen exterior. A front she now understood was a necessary survival tool for her new friend who'd been hurt and had hurt the person closest to her.

Donal and the lads briefly dissected how their first performance had gone over in the Havana Lounge, deciding it had been well received. The Billy Ray Cyrus line dancing number in the second half was a triumph. It allowed Maureen to show off her line dancing moves as she got the stragglers on the dance floor by coaxing them through the 'Achy Breaky Heart' steps. Hopefully, the popularity of The Gamblers' Kenny Rogers tribute act and the band's line-dancing hits repertoire would wipe the slate clean where Donal's ping-pong reputation was concerned. Maureen squirmed, listening in relief when the emergency lifeboat drill/manchild incident wasn't revisited. She quickly moved the conversation along to Cabo, asking what everybody fancied doing on their first day in a Mexican city.

Carole said she was keen to snorkel, and Niall was quick off the mark to say he fancied donning the mask and flippers, too. Davey, who'd a guidebook, had pinpointed a bar dedicated to the Rolling Stones who'd enjoyed sun-drenched, hedonistic holidays in Cabo. He and John were keen to check this out.

Maureen didn't have anything she wanted to do other than meander and soak up the flavour of Mexico. She and Donal were on the same page. It wasn't surprising because they were a team. *Just not team players*, she thought ruefully before speaking up. 'We're luckier than this lot.' She flapped her hand in the direction of fellow passengers.

'Why's that then, Mo?' John asked. 'I mean aside from the obvious.'

Davey – with pastry crumbs stuck to greasy lips – asked, 'What's obvious?'

'We're getting paid to be here,' Donal supplied the answer.

'Good point.' Davey wiped his mouth.

'And,' Maureen continued, 'as contracted entertainers, we've no need to go mad cramming all the sights in because we'll be back again and again and again. We've the luxury of leisurely exploring, picking, and choosing what we do. Well, so long as we're back on the ship before it sets sail. The only thing I absolutely have to do is find an internet café. You're with me there, aren't you, Carole?'

CHAPTER 20

Carole's earlier confidence turned to shiftiness because time was ticking closer to when they'd get off the ship for the first time since walking up the gangplank. Nevertheless, she agreed this was the case.

Donal checked his watch. 'We'd better head back to the cabin and fetch the day pack, Mo.'

'I'll follow you down,' John said. 'I need to put a fresh shirt on.' He wiped at the blob of jam stuck to his front with a napkin, succeeding in spreading the sticky stain.

The others were good to go, having brought their supplies upstairs with them.

'We'll take the lift. Save time, like,' Donal said.

He'd begun walking like a bow-legged gunslinger, Maureen thought as she and John trotted alongside him. 'Who're you trying to kid, Donal McCarthy? It's to save your legs.' She filled John in on Donal's rowing exploits.

Donal wasn't offended as he laughed good naturedly that Maureen had got him worked out. However, seeing the swarm of passengers loitering by the lifts, the laughter died in his throat. He had no choice but to take the stairs, or they'd be waiting an age. He moaned and groaned all the way down.

'It's falling on deaf ears, Donal McCarthy,' Maureen threw over her shoulder.

———*ele*———

It seemed that they'd donned orange life jackets in no time and were being herded off the ship onto a bobbing tender. Excitement swelled with a din of voices, all chatting about what they had planned for their day. They sat elbow to elbow in the boat, steadily motoring toward the harbour. Maureen turned her face to the water, enjoying the tang of cool, salty breeze on her lips as she soaked it all in. Ahead, a lone kayaker paddled lazily through the calm waters close to the bustling waterfront. The marina area teemed with life as restaurants, touts and shopkeepers prepared for the cruise ship deluge.

'Donal, there're palm trees!' The tall, slender trunks, with crowns of fronds, were studded about, adding a holiday vibe to the vista. At home in Howth, Maureen had to make do with the spiky cabbage tree outside the pub on the main street for the seaside holiday vibe.

'So there are, Mo,' Donal said indulgently.

Maureen's eyes travelled beyond the smattering of high-rise buildings to the backdrop of whitewashed Spanish-style homes with terracotta roofs beyond which acrid, cactus-filled hills were in stark contrast to the blue sky. Today would be hers, Donal's and the others' first foray into Mexico. Anticipation saw her begin fidgeting in eagerness to get off the boat and plant her feet on the foreign soil as she conjured up the little she knew of Mexico. Mariachi bands, beans and corn, more beans, cheese, Tequilla, sombreros and pinatas. Noah had had a birthday party pinata once. Maureen shuddered, recalling the grim determination with which those children had smacked the thing to get to the sweets within. They'd been blindfolded, and all the adults had kept a wary distance as the young wans took turns with the big stick.

'Look over there,' Carole said, pointing to where sea otters were basking on a rickety wooden pontoon, taking aim with her camera. Then their boat was bumping against the dock, and they were being helped off. The helpful *Mayan Princess* crew member wished them a wonderful time in Cabo.

'I'm crew too,' Maureen said as she took his hand but there was no time to expand on her role as she was jostled from behind.

The party of six found themselves milling about the hot marina in a sea of sun hats. The smells of sunscreen, cigarettes, and grilling fish filled the air while the shouts of the cowboy-hat-wearing men with Water taxi signs all vying for their business competed with a thumping music beat.

John and Davey announced they would attend the Stones bar they'd mentioned earlier. It was in a nearby square, and they hoped it might have interesting memorabilia to enjoy while sampling local tequila. Maureen wondered whether Kenny might have ever holidayed here in Cabo. She reminded them to hydrate with water and not just tequila because they'd not want banging heads for tonight's performance in the Havana Lounge. Niall and Carole would accompany Maureen and Donal to an internet café and then head off for snorkelling.

Maureen's face was soon aching from all the polite smiling at the touts wanting their business as she mouthed, 'No, thank you.' At the same time, they kept their eyes peeled for a café that wasn't packed out with cruise ship passengers all eager to email their adventures home. They found one with two available consoles a little way behind the marina. Maureen told Donal she'd be sure to include Anna and Louise in her newsy update to ship life. All two days of it.

Carole's shoulders were tense as her fingers hovered over the keyboard she'd sat down in front of. 'My mind's gone blank, Maureen. What should I say?'

'Go straight to the point of the message. You want— Carlos, isn't it?'

Carole confirmed this was his name with a dip of her head.

'You want Carlos's mobile phone number and you should tell your ex-husband to keep your having asked for it to himself.'

'Rob won't say anything if I ask him not to.' Still, her fingers were poised over the keys.

'You can do it, Carole,' Maureen said gently. 'You've got nothing to lose, remember.'

'And maybe everything to gain.'

'Exactly.'

Carole tapped out a brief message, pushing 'send' before she could change her mind.

'Well done.' Maureen smiled, then, including Niall, loitering nearby, said, 'I'm going to be a while with all the news I've got to share. I'd better not forget to let Rosemary and Cathal know how we're getting on. So don't hang about on my part.'

Carole looked at Niall. 'Shall we walk around the waterfront to see if we can't buy a cheap mask and flippers?'

'I can't wait to get in that water,' Niall said.

'Me too,' Carole agreed.

Maureen glanced up to see them smiling in that way that people who are just getting to know one another do when they discover something else they've got in common. In this case, a love of snorkelling. She wasn't sure how much snorkelling Niall had availed himself of, given he usually spent his holidays in Dundalk, County Louth, which didn't lend itself to tropical conditions for the mask and flippers. Still, she'd not say a word and ruin the moment. Unlike Donal, she thought glowering, as he ploughed into the tender scene.

'Well, all I can say is good luck to you both. You couldn't pay me to put a toe in that water and, for your sakes, I hope you've the colourful swimwear on.'

'Why, Donal?' Carole asked, her eyes abruptly torn from Niall to the blustering Donal. She was wearing a loose sundress beneath which the straps of a black swimsuit peeked.

'Well, if it's the black swimsuit you're after wearing, Carole, as I suspect you are, who's to say a shark won't think you're a seal?'

Carole didn't seem phased but then she came from Australia, and everybody knew they'd all manner of nasties waiting to eat you over there. As for Niall, he was staring down at his turquoise swirly board shorts and then, looking up, he scowled at his pal.

'Don't listen to Donal, Carole. They'd not hire the flippers and mask out if Jaws lurked in the shallows.' He took his lady friend by the arm in a masterful way that suggested he'd bop anything on the nose that made a beeline for them in the

CHAPTER 20

water if need be. Then, creating a loose arrangement to catch Maureen and Donal later, perhaps for a drink in one of the waterfront bars around 4.30ish, they headed off searching for snorkelling gear.

'Grand, have fun,' Maureen called after them with a waggle of her fingers while Donal hummed the *Jaws* film music, receiving a rude finger sign from Niall for his efforts.

'Behave, Donal.' Maureen tsked.

Donal grinned but instead of pulling up the seat that Carole had just vacated, he said he might go and wander through the indoor market next door, given Maureen was likely to be a while. Maureen didn't look up from where she was tapping in O'Mara's email address as she promised to find him when she'd finished. The door to the café opened and closed. Then her fingers began flying over the keyboard in her haste to convey everything that had happened between waving Pat, Cindy and the babby Brianna off to finding herself sitting in a poky internet café with an ancient air conditioner unit that sounded like a DC10 plane about to take off. Still and all, she was grateful it was there because, she typed, Cabo was hot.

—ele—

'All done, Mo?' Donal asked as Maureen tracked him down in the market twenty minutes later. She'd found him admiring a t-shirt with a Cabo San Lucas logo set against a technicoloured rainbow palm tree.

'All done.' Maureen smiled, flexing her fingers which ached from the long letter she'd just typed and sent out as a group email. Then, seeing him putting his hand in his shorts pocket for his wallet, she asked, 'Did you haggle?'

'No. I asked the young lady here how much the shirt was, and now I'm about to pay.'

'Oh no, Donal, you've to haggle. It's expected.'

'Is it?'

'It is.'

'You're far more worldly than I am, Mo, what with visiting Vietnam. I expect they haggle there, do they?'

'They do indeed, Donal.'

Haggling, however, did not come naturally to Donal, who bounced back a price fifty cents cheaper than the one in American dollars he'd already been given.

'No, no, Donal.' Maureen shook her head. 'You've got to go in ludicrously low; your woman here will come back ridiculously high, and then you meet in the middle. It's how it works. Isn't that so?' Maureen addressed the woman, staring at them with a surly expression. She gave nothing away.

Ultimately, Donal left it to Maureen who drove a hard bargain and accepted the bagged t-shirt from the now scowling woman, feeling pleased with herself. She'd managed to buy the shirt for a quarter of the initial price Donal had been prepared to pay. Then, seeing a little boy in a singlet and nappy sitting on a mat behind the stall pushing a toy truck around, she felt guilty and elbowed Donal, who yelped, to give the woman what he'd initially agreed to pay.

'Why?'

'Because she needs it more than we do.'

'You're a soft touch, Maureen,' he said, not minding in the least. 'Although you've very pointy elbows, if you don't mind me saying.'

They strolled around the market, checking out the varied wares for sale but Donal's wallet remained in his pocket. They agreed there was no immediate need for Cabo San Lucas fridge magnets; Maureen also didn't need a sarong, given she'd a caftan, and the flip-flops on their feet were perfectly adequate. There was no room to decorate their cabin with traditional Mexican artworks or a storage room to hoard them for their return to Ireland. It was touch and go with the Cabo version of the garden gnome Maureen set her heart on. Donal successfully managed to talk her down by saying he'd feel like the little bearded man with a sombrero clutching a guitar was watching him all the time in their teeny-tiny cruise ship cabin. So, they turned their back on the items piled high in the stuffy marketplace and wandered into the glaring sunshine to stroll along the marina.

Maureen insisted they pause to hydrate, and that's when Donal spotted a Motorbike rental stand; at that exact moment, Maureen noticed the glass-bottomed boat taking a group out. Only it was like no glass-bottomed boat she'd ever seen, not that there were many. This one, however, was completely see-through. A transparent boat. It was putting her in mind of the invisible plane Wonder Woman used to whizz about in on the seventies television programme, only a boat version, obviously. To head out to sea in one of them immediately became underlined with red pen on her bucket list.

'I used to have a little moped back in the sixties, Mo. I loved it. Shall we hire one for an hour? I'll drive; you can ride pillion.'

'Sure you know yourself, Donal, you wouldn't hire a motorbike when wearing flip-flops at the beach in Howth. And we'd be quick to advise the children against doing so, especially in a foreign country. People go on holiday and take risks they'd never take at home.'

'Tis true enough, Mo, but what the children don't know won't hurt them, and it's a harmless, old, slow poke moped, not a motorbike.' Donal's eyes sparkled with a lust for adventure.

It was very attractive that sparkle, Maureen thought. One of them had to be sensible, though. 'Would our insurance even cover us?'

'It was a comprehensive policy, Mo. I'll pootle along so I will, and look, there's helmets.'

Maureen could see the naked longing on Donal's face. Even though the lure of a see-through boat trip was tugging, she knew compromise was the key to a successful relationship.

'Sure, we could hire the little motorbike for an hour and then take a spin out on yer boat over there.'

'What boat?'

'The see-through boat.'

'Tis a very small boat, and why's it see-through, Mo? That's not normal.'

'So you can see all the lovely, colourful fish and coral. Sure, look, it's perfectly safe. See that couple there are off the ship? They're taking a spin on it.'

'Jaysus, yer woman nearly tipped it over,' Donal exclaimed seeing the boat bobbing precariously. Then, looking at Maureen, who was staring longingly at the boat, envisaging all the vibrant sea life the likes of which she'd not see in Howth's Claremont Beach, he made a slow whistling noise through his clenched teeth and reluctantly agreed to a tour.

Maureen insisted they shake on it and no sooner had they done so than Donal was hot-footing it over to the motorbikes. It was the fastest Maureen had seen him move since his return from the gym. It might be the fastest she'd ever seen him move full stop! And, flip-flopping in his wake, she half-expected to see a scorch mark on the ground. What was she letting herself in for?

Chapter 21

♥

It took Donal three attempts to throw a leg over the moped. He'd hired the bike for an hour after flashing his driver's licence like an FBI agent at the young man manning the stand. A piece of paper had needed to be signed before he was handed two helmets and a set of keys. Maureen had only half been joking when she said he was signing his life away. Now, they were waiting to get the show on the road. 'This gym malarkey is no good for men over sixty, Mo. I'm telling you, it does more harm than good. It might help if you count me down.'

Maureen rolled her eyes. 'On the count of five. Ready?'

Donal was like a man eyeing the high jump, grim determination glinting in his eyes, fists clenched by his sides as he gave Maureen the nod. 'As I'll ever be.'

'Five, four, three, two, two and a half, one!'

Donal worked through the pain to leap majestically on the moped. Once he'd recovered from the exertion, he raised his arms victoriously.

Maureen, holding the helmets, had their hats stashed in her backpack. She stole a glance at Donal's bare legs and then at her own. 'It would have been nice to have had the protective leathers to wear.'

'In this heat?' Donal held his hand out for one of the helmets. 'We'd have got very sweaty, so.'

Maureen passed the helmet over and then slipped the other onto her head, feeling slightly claustrophobic and hot. 'You've a point there, I suppose, Donal, it is hot.' Still and all, she liked to look the part, and biker girls and their fellas wore leathers. She wasn't sure about moped girls and their fellas, though. Donal secured his helmet, then helped Maureen with hers, giving her a wink as he said, 'Climb on board my ride.'

Maureen giggled, 'Ooh, saucy.' Then, seeing the tiny piece of seat protruding behind Donal's backside said, 'Where am I supposed to sit? There's no room.'

'I'll shuffle up. Sure, we'll be grand.' Donal did so until he was all but perched on the handlebars.

Maureen was eager for the off because the sooner Donal had done a few circuits of Cabo and relived his glory days, the sooner they'd sit in that see-through boat sailing out to observe the rainbow-coloured fish. So, despite her misgivings, she clambered on the back, fidgeting about trying to ensure that half of her backside was on the bike and not hanging off the end. She wrapped her arms around Donal's waist. 'You promise you'll go slowly?'

'Of course I will. Are you sorted?'

'I think so.'

That was good enough for Donal, and he turned the key. The moped roared into life, surprisingly gutsy for such a small bike. Unfortunately, at that moment, Maureen felt a stinging on her thigh and, glancing down, saw a mosquito having lunch. She released her grip on Donal to swipe it off just as he twisted the throttle and shot forward. The suddenness saw her sail right off the rear of the moped to land on her back, cushioned by her backpack and then floundering like a tortoise trying to right itself. She gave up: lying there, winded and blinking up at the blue sky in surprise at where she found herself. At the

CHAPTER 21   147

same time, oblivious that she was no longer hanging off the back, Donal zipped off down the road.

'Are you alright?' a familiar voice was asking.

Maureen found herself looking up into the face of Tony, the Manchild. Was she hallucinating?

'Give the woman some space,' he ordered the curious passersby who'd stopped to watch the unfolding drama.

Meanwhile, Maureen, getting over her shock, managed to sit upright and declared to the onlookers, 'There's nothing to see here. No broken bones.' She'd a strong sense of deja vu flashing back to the mule incident in Santorini but that was then, and this was now, so addressing Tony, she said, 'Would you help me stand up, please?'

He thrust his hand toward her, and she grabbed it with hers. It was definitely real, as were the rope-like sinews standing to attention in his arm as he hauled her to her feet. 'Thank you.' She let go of his hand and jiggled her arms and legs, realising she was missing a flip-flop. Then, she threw in a couple of squats to check that everything was as it should be. Aside from a bruised bottom, she was fine. She was still wearing her helmet; she took it off and scanned the horizon, spying Donal a little way down the road. He'd pulled over to the side and was casting about bewilderedly, apparently only just having realised he was riding solo. She waved out and, seeing her, he threw his arms out in a 'What's going on?' gesture before nosing the bike around to make a U-turn.

'You're not hurt then,' Tony, the Manchild, stated somewhat flatly.

'Are you disappointed?'

'No, but I'm your man if you'd a slight sprain or something. I've not long finished my first aid training.'

'Well, I'm tickety-boo.' She checked on Donal, who was still waiting for a break in the traffic, and decided this was her chance to set the record straight. 'But I think you and I have got off on the wrong foot, young man.'

Tony took a wary step backwards, looking vulnerable in his colourful singlet and tight little shorts.

'I am not nor have I ever been a cougar. I'm the mother of a son older than yourself, and I'm in a very happy relationship with Donal McCarthy.'

'You mean the Kenny Rogers look-a-like fella who just took off on a moped like a bat out of hell and left you for dead?'

'I don't think he realised I was no longer on the back but yes, that's him.' Seeing doubt flickering across Tony's face, she decided to fess up. 'I only sang the "We've Got Tonight" song in the lift to annoy you because you annoyed me trampling all over myself and Donal's dream to sing on a stage as big as the one in the Grand Theatre. It was on my bucket list, so it was, and you were very obnoxious, shooing us off like so.'

Tony shook his head. 'But you chased me.'

'Only so I could explain the misunderstanding.'

'So, you're saying I crushed your dream and you sang a very suggestive song in the lift to wind me up?' Tony was beginning to squirm.

That was a little dramatic, and her behaviour sounded very childish relayed like so, but yes, that was about the sum of it. Maureen would roll with it, she decided, nodding. 'Crushed it into teeny-tiny smithereens.'

Tony sniffed, 'I know what it's like to have your dream crushed. My dream was never the cruise ship circuit. I wanted to see my name in lights in London's West End. I nearly made it, too. I was this close to getting a part in *Cats*.' He showed her how close with his thumb and forefinger, then made paws of his hands and pretended to lick them.

'Very good. I'd have given you the part.' So long as it was a hungry stray he was auditioning for. He'd be no good as a plump domestic cat. The only thing Maureen knew about the musical – other than it was about cats, obviously – was the "Memory" song. It was very haunting so. She was more of a dog person and had never fancied seeing it. Now, if your

Lloyd Webber wan had written a musical called *Dogs*, she'd have been in like Flynn. 'And sure, you're young enough not to give up on your dreams. A person should never give up on their dreams, young man. Think of the *Mayan Princess* as a stepping stone. I can feel it in my water. You'll see your name in lights, Tony.'

'You can?' Tony's eyes were eager and full of hope, and then they narrowed. 'How did you know my name?'

'I thought we'd moved past all that. I've not been stalking you and Tony, if you don't mind me saying, it's a very high opinion you have of yourself. I overheard you and your friend talking. And, yes, I can feel it in my water. If my daughters were here, they'd tell you I get all sorts of funny feelings in my water.'

'I'm sorry for trampling all over your dream.'

'Tis alright,' Maureen said.

'You know my name but I don't know yours.'

'Maureen. Maureen O'Mara from Dublin.'

'Tony Smith. I'm from London, but my stage name is Antony Garcia. My mum's maiden name. She's Italian.'

'Well then, Tony Antony Smith Garcia, shall we shake hands and pretend we're meeting for the first time?' Tony held his hand out and Maureen shook it vigorously. 'Nice to meet you, Tony.'

'And you, Maureen.'

Donal roared up alongside them. Well, it was more of an annoying whine, truth be told, and he stilled the engine to ask, 'Mo, why did you get off? You should have just said that you didn't want to go for a ride. I was frightened when I realised you weren't on the back.'

'I didn't get off, you great big eejit. I fell off when you took off like you were in that film *Easy Rider*, and the "Born to be Wild" music was playing. Tony here came to my rescue. Tony meet Donal.'

The two men nodded a greeting, and then Donal swung his stunned gaze in Maureen's way. 'You fell off, you say? Are you hurt?'

'Not at all. Well, I've a bruised bottom, but I'm grand apart from that.'

'Thank goodness.'

'But Donal if you think I'm getting back on that thing with you, you can think again.'

Donal made no argument as he removed his helmet and thanked Tony for coming to her aid.

Maureen suspected Donal's attitude might have been altogether different had it been Captain Franco who'd been the hero of the hour.

Tony glanced at his watch and announced he was meeting friends in a bar. 'Would you like to join me? The bar does a mean burger.'

'No, you're grand, Tony lad. Mo and I have a date in a see-through boat. We'll take a rain check, though: maybe next time.'

Maureen bobbed her head to the raincheck.

They said their goodbyes, and Donal wheeled the moped back to the stand, meekly handing in the helmets and key. A quick search for Maureen's missing flip-flop ensued, and they found it hanging off a nearby cactus. Donal attempted to bend to help her slip it on her foot like she was Cinderella. Only his sore muscles wouldn't allow it. Maureen told him it was the thought that counted as she shoved her foot back in the flip-flop. Then, linking arms, they decided to put the moped debacle behind them and embrace the see-through boat experience. Maureen pretended she couldn't feel Donal's arm trembling. She appreciated his willingness to do something out of his comfort zone for her benefit.

'That was gas!' Donal gushed about their ocean excursion while they waited in line to board the *Mayan Princess*. Niall and Carole were in front of them, glowing from too much time in the sun, hair bedraggled and salty but with all body parts intact.

Carole had already told them about their snorkelling adventure, which they'd thoroughly enjoyed.

'We did see a reef shark,' Niall informed Donal, who shuddered. 'They're more scared of us than we are them.'

'If you say so.' Donal didn't look convinced.

'Who'd have thought fish would come in so many colours,' Carole said. 'It's a whole other world under the water.'

'I liked the parrotfish best of all with their rainbow colours. What about you, Mo?' Donal asked.

Maureen, unusually quiet but no longer green, couldn't have given a toss whether there'd been a flipping peacock fish swimming about in the water. She muttered something non-committal.

'How are you feeling now?' Donal asked, passing the water bottle her way. 'Here, drink some of this and put some fluids back into your system.'

Maureen took a dutiful but wary sip, tuning Donal and his *Finding Nemo* saga out. In her mind, she fetched her bucket list and drew a big red line through sailing in a see-through boat twice. She jotted it down under a new list headed, 'Over My Dead Body Will I Do That Again'. Riding pillion on a moped with Donal came in at number two.

The excursion had not got well on her part because no sooner had she sat down in the boat than her stomach had begun to churn. She'd found it not just unnatural but unnerving to be able to see the water beneath them like so and had quickly become hypnotised by the waves they were puttering over. Around the halfway mark between the marina and the arch all the boats made a beeline for she'd wound up hanging over the side of the ship feeling like she was dying. Donal, however, was in his applecart. He'd been thrilled by the entire experience, exclaiming delightedly over the schools of fishes swimming under the boat in between assuring her she'd find her sea legs. He would never know how close he'd come to being pushed overboard when he'd rocked the boat further by waving out to fellow sight-seers on the water as though they were long-lost family.

Maureen had not found her sea legs, nor had she ever been so relieved to step back onto dry land in all her days.

Donal was still harping on about the see-through boat experience hours later as Maureen, refusing to engage, rubbed the Deep Heat into his tight calf muscles in their cabin. They'd an hour before The Gamblers' evening show. Despite her earlier vow, she'd bought a tube of the smelly wintergreen stuff from the ship's pharmacy once back on the boat. This was because Donal assured her he had learned his lesson about not doing the warm-up before exercising. However, it was mostly because she'd decided the cruise ship passengers had not paid good money to see a bow-legged Kenny Rogers look-a-like singing his biggest hits.

Chapter 22

♥

Meanwhile, back in Dublin...

Bronagh finished checking the Belfast businessman out of room seven with an efficiency honed from her long service behind O'Mara's reception desk. She graced him with her high-beam smile as she waved him off and wished him well in his meetings before calling out to Freya, her voice suggesting it was urgent. Since the twins' arrival, Aisling had realised she needed to loosen her grip on running the guesthouse, and Freya was her right-hand woman. She was currently amid her morning routine next door in the guests' lounge, replenishing the tea and coffee sachets, tidying magazines, and plumping cushions. A creature of habit, Freya's expression was disgruntled as she appeared in reception to see what couldn't wait a minute longer.

'There's an email after pinging through for Aisling and Moira from Maureen,' Bronagh explained. 'I tried ringing upstairs to let them know, but the phone's engaged.' Both women were aware of Kiera's latest trick. The toddler had taken to clambering onto a chair to pick up the phone. She'd hold an animated one-way conversation and then hang up, but she'd not mastered properly putting the phone back on the hook. The more Moira told her not to do it, the more Kiera seized every back-turned opportunity that came her way. You never knew whether someone was actually on the phone or not. 'You know yourself how they've been carrying on as if they've been orphaned since their mammy and Donal left: they'll want to read it pronto.'

Freya nodded and, given she had a streak of the fecky brown-noser in her – according to Moira – she was eager to be the one to run upstairs to tell the sisters. 'I'll go up now and tell them to come down. I don't mind watching the little ones for a while, seeing as Tom and Quinn are out for a run.' If she wondered why Bronagh didn't print off a copy for her to pass on, she didn't ask.

'That's very good of you, Freya.' Bronagh was just as keen for an update on how life aboard a cruise ship was treating Maureen and Donal. She fancied the idea of a cruise for her and Leonard's honeymoon. Mrs Flaherty, too, would want to hear Maureen's update because she wrote a good letter. The sort that made you feel like a fly on the wall.

'Not at all,' Freya said, already heading for the stairs. All the staff were fond of the O'Mara children and keen for any excuse to cuddle them, especially the twins at that plump baby stage. Where Kiera was concerned, though, you'd want to watch you weren't wearing white when she wrapped herself around you. Lately, she seemed to have always had her hand shoved in something she shouldn't. Bronagh had wound up with peanut butter handprints all over her cream blouse the last time the toddler had sat on her knee. She kept her mammy on her toes, that was for sure!

Hearing Freya's light footfall on the stairs, Bronagh hit 'print' on the computer and swivelled in her seat, waiting for the printer to spit the letter out. All four pages of it. Then, getting up, she headed past the storage cupboard to the top of the stairs leading down to the basement kitchen and dining area to call out to Mrs Flaherty that Maureen had sent an email if she wanted to come and hear all the news. The breakfast service was finished but the mouth-watering aroma of bacon lingered as the cook banged about in the kitchen, clearing up for the day. She appeared at the bottom of the stairs, red in the face from all her rub-a-dub-dubbing to say she'd be up in two ticks.

Meanwhile, having reached the top floor, Freya tapped on the door of the O'Mara family apartment. She could hear an almighty din coming from within and knocked again to ensure she'd been heard. A frazzled Moira opened the door.

'How're you, Freya?'

'Grand, Moira.' Freya didn't bother asking how Moira was as it was apparent how she was faring. 'Bronagh sent me up to tell you and Aisling your mammy's after emailing. I'm volunteering to watch the children if you two want to head downstairs to read her letter together.'

Moira looked tempted to run off downstairs without so much as a backward glance, however she beckoned Freya in. 'You might regret that offer. Kiera and the twins are in the middle of band practice.'

Freya trailed behind Moira, the noise growing ever louder, into the sitting room where Aisling was at the table with a calculator and spreadsheet in front of her. 'Bronagh tried to ring but I think your phone is off the hook again,' Freya shouted over the top of the children.

Moira checked it and pulled a face. 'It was. Thanks, Freya. Kiera, I'm beginning to sound like a broken record. You're to stop playing with the telephone, do you hear me?'

Sitting on the kitchen floor with a couple of upturned pots in front of her, Kiera was too busy smacking them with the wooden spoon like she was Charlie Watts from the Rolling Stones to care. Meanwhile, the twins sat on either side of her in their nappies and vests, taking turns emitting high-pitched squeals.

'They're singing.' Aisling looked up from her task. 'I think I've potentially got a pair of opera singers in the making. Listen to how they hit those high notes.'

Freya cocked an ear, winced and demurred to her boss, 'Oh, definitely bright futures there, Aisling.' Her eyes travelled past Aisling to the many panes of glass in the Georgian windows, expecting to see them buckling and shattering.

'Fecky brown-noser,' Moira said under her breath, adding loudly, 'They're shredding my nerves and potentially going to give me a migraine if they keep it up. Can't you jam a rusk in their gobs, Ash?'

Aisling ignored her sister as she asked Freya what had brought her upstairs. Upon hearing there was a message from their mammy, she heaved a relieved sigh. 'At last. We thought they were MIA.' She pushed her chair back from the table and got up.

'MIA?' Freya asked.

'Missing in Action. It's been three days since they last made contact.'

'Well, I suppose Maureen and Donal have been in the middle of the ocean, so they couldn't get in touch until they reached one of the cruise ship's stops,' Freya appeased.

'Where there's a will, there's a way,' Moira stated, backing her sister. 'Sure, in days of old, they used carrier pigeons. She could have strapped a message to a seagull and sent it on its way.'

Freya wasn't sure whether Moira was joking or not. Nor was she sure as the sisters headed out the door and Moira's voice drifted back, 'Sure you don't mind if myself and Aisling head out to a day spa after we've read what Mammy has to say, do you?'

She tittered nervously, looking anxiously to where Kiera was now waving the spoon at her baby cousins like a conductor.

The door banged shut before she could reply.

Aisling and Moira just about tripped over one another in their haste to get downstairs. 'You shouldn't wind Freya up like so,' Aisling admonished, reaching the first floor and pausing to tell Ita a message from Maureen had arrived.

'You're welcome to come and listen to what she has to say.'

'Thanks, but I'd better crack on here. We've had a good few guests check out this morning, so I've a lot to get through. Bronagh can fill me in on all the news when I clock off later.'

Aisling and Moira exchanged glances as Ita returned to dragging her hoover down the hall. It was a look that questioned, not for the first time, whether this was the same girl they had nicknamed Idle Ita, who'd been employed solely because Mammy was friends with her mammy. She'd turned over a new leaf when she'd met a nice fella and started her veterinary nursing course, fitting it in around her housekeeping duties at O'Mara's.

The sisters found Bronagh and Mrs Flaherty eagerly awaiting them, and the honours fell on Aisling to read the email out loud. Mrs Flaherty and Moira sank into the sofa to listen. At the same time, Bronagh scooted her chair close to where Aisling stood in front of the brochures, checking the email pages to ensure they were in order.

'Moira, if I close my eyes, don't think I've fallen asleep. I'm soaking in the ambience of what Maureen's got to say. I want to feel like I'm on the cruise ship with her and Donal,' Mrs Flaherty said.

'Three's a crowd, don't you know?' Moira received a 'cheeky mare' response from the breakfast cook.

Aisling cleared her throat, glancing up to ensure she had all their attention; she cleared her throat again.

'Ash, it's not the reading of the will. Get on with it, would you, or I'll do it.'

Aisling began to read, and by the time she'd reached the 'All my love, Mammy and Donal' part, her voice was hoarse.

'Doesn't it sound wonderful?' Mrs Flaherty was the first to speak up. 'An entire station dedicated just for the omelette making. Imagine it.' She shook her head.

'Those Blue Lagoon cocktails sounded delicious,' Bronagh said. 'Although I'm partial to a Strawberry Daiquiri on my holidays.'

'Imagine lying poolside soaking up the sun while the children are entertained in a Kids' club.' Moira was entranced by the idea and mentally counting down the days between now and their holiday.

'Imagine eating whatever you want at the Lido Buffet, whenever you want and not having to cook or wash a single dish. Just think, Moira. That will be us in a month.'

'They're having a grand time,' Bronagh said.

'Do you think they miss us?' Aisling wondered out loud.

'Bound to,' Mrs Flaherty replied reassuringly.

'I miss her and Donal,' Aisling said. 'Roll on the cruise.'

'Me too and I can't wait either,' Moira agreed, and then she frowned. 'What I want to know, though, was what the Golden Arch thing in Cabo was all about? It sounds like she spotted a floating McDonalds. Now that I'd like to see.'

Chapter 23

♥

Day 4 - Port of Call, Mazatlán

Maureen and Donal had eaten a leisurely breakfast, after which they decided to watch their arrival into the historic city of Mazatlán's port from the *Mayan Princess*'s railings. So, leaving their table in the morning-sun-dappled restaurant, they made their way out to the deck to find the stillness of an hour or so ago had been replaced by a gusty wind. Maureen's hair whipped about her face as they found a spot alongside the railings amongst all the other passengers eager to watch the enormous ship being guided into the port by tugboats and for their first glimpse of the Mexican city.

It quickly became apparent that they weren't docking in a quaint fishing harbour but rather a busy hub where another cruise line's ship was already moored for the day, along with cargo ships and larger fishing vessels. The scene was an industrial hive of comings and goings. Beyond the coastline, the rugged Sierra Madre mountains framed a glittering city skyline. To the right of the harbour, a large lighthouse stood sentry. Maureen was excited for the few hours they had to explore as she dug out her camera and took aim.

'Look, there's the Malécon, Donal.' She liked how the word for the sweep of coastal promenade stretching as far as the eye could see rolled off her tongue. 'I'm looking forward to strolling along that. Although if it's as blowy as this onshore, we'll want to keep a tight hold of our hats.' The promenade was one of the longest in the world, according to the *Mayan Princess*'s daily newsletter.

As the boat juddered into its allocated berth, the crowds dispersed and they pushed off from the railing, going to meet the others as they'd arranged outside the Grand Theatre. Maureen saw Tony mincing past and waved out. She was pleased to see him wave back with equal enthusiasm. He'd meant what he said yesterday, then.

Sitting next to Carole in the theatre, waiting for their slot to be called, Maureen could sense the Australian woman's edginess. She hoped she'd have loads of news from home when she opened her Hotmail account and was wondering how the family was getting on as they got up and inched out of the theatre. In single file, they went down the stairs to join the orderly line, waiting to pass their bags through the security scanner.

Soon, the party of six were walking down the gangplank, and a shuttle bus waited to take them and as many others who could squeeze on board to the terminal building. Donal told anyone listening that he was keen to wander about the old town. There was a murmured agreement that this sounded grand but, still, no firm plans were shored up other than that and Carole's input of needing to find an internet café.

A welcoming Mariachi band was in full swing as they stepped off the bus and into the terminal building.

'Arriba!' Maureen cried. 'I wish I had a set of castanets or my tambourine to join them!' She reached for her camera and passed it to John, who took her and Donal's picture with the traditional musicians. Carole, Niall and Davey, who'd not had much time for souvenir shopping in Cabo, had already moved off to admire the colourful wares at the smattering of well-located market stalls. It was impossible to exit the terminal without walking past them. Smiling vendors greeted them as they stopped to browse.

By the time they stepped out into the hot sun, where lines of taxis were whisking tourists off to explore the delights of Mazatlán, Maureen was the proud owner of eight woven friendship bracelets. She had four on each wrist, having haggled the colourful accessories down to a mutually satisfactory price. Carole, who'd been to Bali on holiday, knew the need to bargain back and forth. However, Niall, John and Davey needed the rundown on not accepting the asking price. Maureen reminded them of her trip to Vietnam with Moira, where the art of haggling was necessary in the markets. 'Only don't get carried away because these people have a living to make,' she'd added, recalling her conscious-pricing moment in Cabo. Then, as though Moira was haunting her, she could almost hear her youngest daughter's voice in her ear as she wandered along with the beads from all her new necklaces clacking about her neck.

'You've not learned the art of not buying things that will look ridiculous back home though, Mammy,' she was saying in Maureen's head.

'Go away,' Maureen said.

'Did you say something, Mo?' Donal asked. Or at least she thought it was Donal. It was hard to tell, given he, Niall, and Davey looked like the three Amigos, all wearing matching straw beach sombreros.

'I was talking to myself, Donal.'

'Grand.'

Maureen shifted the carry bag from one hot little hand to the other. Her family was never far from her thoughts and she'd bought six Huipils, the traditional white cotton blouses with splashes of embroidery, for all the grown-up girls. She couldn't wait to take a family photograph, picturing the girls in their chaste blouses and blue jeans.

She'd sort the lads out next time around. Perhaps they'd like a t-shirt with Mazatlán printed on the front like Donal had stuffed into the carry bag, announcing his desire to own a t-shirt from each of their three destinations to wear on rotation throughout the cruise. Or better yet, white cotton shirts! Then everybody could wear white tops and blue jeans for the family photo. Carole, more timid than Maureen despite her previous experience, had paid too much in Maureen's opinion for a pair of silver dangly earrings and a leather purse. John, however, had been a duck-to-water bartering for the leather belt with the big silver buckle that looked very cowboyish and would work well for their Haybales and Hoedown evening. Maureen would put him right if he opted to wear the belt with his chino trousers. It was a look that wouldn't work and, given that his daughter wasn't here to tell him, it would be up to her to say it was a fashion crime.

Given the volumes of people milling about the Malécon, there was no chance of getting lost. Davey had his nose buried in the guidebook he'd brought. Every now and then, he'd emerge from it to give them an insight into the city they decided to wander into rather than take a taxi, much to Donal's angst. The consensus had been they could do with stretching their legs and working off the sins of the Lido Buffet, not to mention all the cocktails they'd consumed.

Maureen frowned while watching the man she loved, who was a few steps ahead. She deduced he was the Amigo in the middle from the waddle, thinking how he looked like he'd an unfortunate case of the chafing. He was still suffering for his gym sins. She bet Kenny didn't strut about bandy-legged on his holidays. Ah well, at least the cruise passengers they'd been brought on board to entertain weren't likely to recognise him as frontman for The Gamblers under his sombrero.

Their group followed the lanyard-wearing trickle, trooping toward the old town. It wasn't long before they left the gusty but cooling wind blowing down the rocky shoreline for a sleepy square. The squalling gulls were replaced with nosy pigeons.

'Plaza Machado,' Davey announced proudly as though he were the Mayor of Mazatlán, coming to a standstill in the square where the smell of grilling fish and cigars clung to the air. There wasn't even a whisper of breeze rustling the palm tree fronds or leaves on the trees offering blessed shade in the square. The plaza was surrounded by pastel colonial buildings home to shops and cafés whose outdoor tables were covered with red chequered cloths. Children played in and around a Rotunda, and old men sat under leafy arbours and played chess. The atmosphere was convivial and welcoming.

'I'm parched,' John announced.

'We'll not find a better spot for a cool drink and people-watching than this,' Donal said.

Niall and Davey were already moving toward a café with an empty table big enough to accommodate them.

Maureen, however, had seen a sign for an internet café in one of the lanes spidering off the square and she nudged Carole, pointing over at it. 'Shall we?'

Carole called out to Niall, 'Would you mind getting me a lemonade? Maureen and I are going to head over there and use the internet. We won't be long.'

'Not a bother,' Niall said, oblivious to what hung on the line for Carole. Once she had Carlos's mobile number, she'd have no excuse for not calling and trying to make peace. Donal echoed Niall's sentiment when Maureen put in her order.

The two women were assailed by a fog of cigarette smoke from three young people at various terminals chuffing away and an underlying whiff of something greasy as they stepped inside the café.

'At least it's cool,' Maureen muttered, sorting out payment with the bored young woman behind the counter. They had their choice of computers, and Carole settled in front of one of the screens while Maureen sat at the monitor beside her. The women got busy entering their details.

Maureen saw she'd had several messages come in since yesterday. One was from Aisling, and the other was from Roisin. Rosemary Farrell had been in touch, as had Donal's Louise, but there was nothing from Pat. She wished Donal had come to the café with her now, but she supposed she could ask for Louise's message to be printed off. She was eager to read them all but knew she couldn't concentrate until Carole checked hers and, while waiting, she crossed her fingers under the desk.

'Rob's sent through the mobile number,' Carole said a second later, seemingly reading Maureen's mind.

'Grand.' Maureen didn't want to give Carole wiggle room because putting it off wouldn't make it any easier. 'What's the time difference between Sydney and Mexico?'

'Um, let me work it out. Okay, so it's one o'clock here which means,' Carole's voice trailed off, and her lips moved silently. 'It's seven in the morning in Sydney. I don't want to ring when Emma's likely to be home, though,' she was quick to add.

'Fair play. I saw a phone box near the terminal. You could always try ringing in a few hours before we return to the ship.'

Carole nodded but said nothing.

'I've a few messages to read if you want to find the lads for that lemonade.'

'I'll wait,' Carole said, 'I'm due to write to a couple of my teaching friends anyway.'

CHAPTER 23   165

The hours spent in the charming city of Mazatlán, where they'd not ventured further than the old town, had flown by. They'd been spent in a flurry of more souvenir shopping, photograph taking and generally soaking up of the different sights, sounds and smells of a foreign port. The group were cleaning up a late lunch of fresh fish and discussing the city's majestic, yellow-hued cathedral when Davey shot out of his seat. He gestured for the rest of them to do the same or they'd miss the cliff divers at El Clavadista.

It was too warm to be herded along, so they were all grumbling, doing their best to keep up with the drummer, who could move surprisingly fast when it came to some things. However, all moans of hot and bothered discontent ceased as they reached the rocky outcrop on the Malécon in time to see an adonis arcing through the air, a bronze bird soaring briefly before diving into the frothing surf below. A gasp sounded from the crowd, followed by cheers and applause when the diver bobbed up and swam over to the base of the rocks. Several spectators surged forward to press money upon him, and Maureen pushed Donal forward.

'Look up there.' Carole, standing next to Maureen, pointed to another young adonis waiting at the cliff's top. Once sure he had the crowd's attention, he paused to pray before taking his turn at the point where the rock dropped away, adding to the 'will he, won't he?' suspense.

'That's nothing to be sniffed at you. Sure, it's forty-five feet; they're jumping off. According to my book, it's all in the timing,' Davey informed them as Maureen hissed he was to put his hand in his pocket this time for the diver. Another young man was already clambering lithely up the rock face.

Maureen cupped her hands either side of her mouth and called up. 'Be careful!' Then, turning to Carole said, 'Think of their poor mammies sitting at home wondering whether they'll come home from work. I can't imagine waving Pat out the door, knowing he was off to make a living by jumping off the Cliffs of Moher for tourists. Donal, take the camera. I can't look.' Maureen passed the camera and covered her eyes, but she couldn't help herself; she had to peek.

A throng of weary cruise ship passengers filed past Maureen and Carole, who'd waved the lads on ahead to the boat, explaining Carole had a call home to make and Maureen would wait for her. The two women were standing outside a phone box on the Malécon waiting for the woman yabbering away inside the booth to hurry up and end her call. The wind had dropped, and the sun was still hot. Maureen fanned herself with the bag containing the postcards. Once she was sitting in the shade on the Lido Deck with a Blue Lagoon, she'd write on the cards, filling in those she'd promised to keep updated from her various groups about the delights of Mazatlán. She could post them tomorrow from Puerto Vallarta.

First things first, though. Right now, Carole had a life-changing phone call to make, and the longer they stood here getting hot and bothered the more anxious the poor woman was getting. She'd make her thumb sore chewing on her nail like so. Maureen thought that a pianist needed her hands in tip-top form, decided enough was enough and, reaching forward, she was about to tap on the window impatiently. The woman chose that moment to hang up and bustle out of the box, pausing to hold the door open for Carole who froze. Maureen gently steered her toward the booth, thanking the woman with a *Mayan Princess* lanyard around her neck. She nodded and hurried off toward the terminal.

'I'm here if you need me,' Maureen said as Carole wedged her foot in the door.

'What do I say?' Anxiety was imprinted on her face.

'You say what's on your heart,' Maureen replied.

'What's on my heart,' Carole repeated, removing her foot and closing the door, leaving Maureen chewing on her own thumbnail. She watched as her Australian friend slotted her visa card into the machine and picked up the phone, tapping out the digits scribbled down on a piece of paper.

'Good luck,' Maureen silently mouthed.

Chapter 24

At this rate, the ship would sail off into the sunset without them, Maureen thought, more concerned about Carole's phone call, continuing to clock up monetary minutes on her visa card and hating to think what her conversation was costing. Still, what price did you put on family? And if Carole was mending bridges, then it would be worth every penny. The length of the call must mean things were going well because if Carlos wasn't interested in what his partner's mammy had to say he'd have given her short shrift.

Maureen yawned. The sun made her sleepy, and her legs were aching from all the standing about feeling surplus to requirements. She decided to wait out the remainder of the call a short way down the Malécon on the bench seat overlooking the water. Walking toward it, Maureen barely registered that the flux of passengers returning to the ship had turned into a sporadic trickle. She was more concerned with taking the weight off, and the fine spray of cooling salt water as the surf hit the rocks in front of where she'd planted herself was gratefully received.

Her mind turned to home. It was early days, but she wondered how Roisin was getting on running the yoga classes without her and Donal there to pick Noah up from school when needed. Her eldest daughter's email had said everything was fine, but what was the point in Roisin telling her if they weren't? It wasn't as if she could help being this far away. What about Aisling and Moira? How were they faring with their reliance on their mammy and Donal where last-minute drop-offs of the twins or toddler Kiera were concerned? They'd certainly feel their absence. Perhaps it would give them a better appreciation of how much she and Donal did for them.

Oh, she did miss them! Pooh, too, who Rosemary assured her was enjoying his holiday with her and Cathal. All the emails she'd hungrily scanned today had been full of everyday life in Ireland, which was carrying on as usual. It was a funny thing, life, Maureen mused, suspecting that while The Gamblers, herself and Donal might have stepped out of routine for a short time, they'd step back into it and feel as though they'd never been away upon their return. This was why it was necessary to soak everything up, which was what she intended to do, Maureen thought, scanning the seemingly endless blue horizon.

So deep in thought was she that when Carole finally tapped her on the shoulder, she shot up in the air.

'Sorry!' Carole apologised with a pink flush to her cheeks. 'I seem to be making a habit of startling you. Thank you for waiting for me, Maureen. I'll probably have to remortgage the house when I get home to pay for that phone call!'

Maureen tried to read her body language for clues and was about to ask how the conversation had gone when a mournful ship's horn rang out. The words dried on her lips as she exchanged a panicked glance with Carole. Carole lifted her wrist and, squinting against the sun, read the time out loud before springing into action. She grabbed Maureen's hand, hauling her off the seat and shouting, 'Run!'

The shuttle was no longer waiting to transport passengers. The two women legged it across the hot tarmac, arriving in a sweaty rush at the gangplank where a ship's security officer, who'd seen them running toward the boat, waited with a walkie-talkie to escort them on board the *Mayan Princess*.

'Sorry,' Maureen mumbled for what felt like the tenth time, flashing her passport as her bag was checked by the security team, who'd been all smiles as they left the boat earlier but were now surly.

'It's my fault,' Carole said to the unimpressed-looking Access Control Officer, scanning her lanyard and ushering her through.

Maureen felt like a collared criminal suddenly granted freedom as she was swept through the security checks to the freedom of the corridor beyond.

'Let me do the talking,' Carole said out the corner of her mouth as a po-faced Donal and Niall stepped forward from the shadows where they'd been waiting anxiously.

Her mild-mannered Donal looked fit to burst, Maureen thought, bracing herself.

'Jaysus wept, Mo! Niall and I were about to jump ship. You two had us worried sick that something terrible had happened.' He ran through the list of all possible scenarios, his and Niall's money being on a rogue wave having swept the two women straight off the Malécon out to sea. 'I've been pacing back and forth here, wondering what I'd tell the family. 'I left your mammy in Mazatlán with our Australian friend, and they vanished'? 'Whoopsie.'

Niall was tapping his watch as he blustered, 'Carole, you're due on in the Atrium in twenty minutes. Talk about cutting it fine, girl.'

'I think the pair of you just knocked ten years off our life expectancy,' Donal huffed.

'Blame me.' Carole was still trying to catch her breath from their cross-country sprint. 'The phone call I had to make was important. And I promise I'll explain it all later but, right now, I've a show to do and if I don't have a quick shower first I'll be booed off my piano.'

CHAPTER 24

Maureen bent over, hands on her knees, puffing, listening to her Aussie twang, thinking she sounded giddy. Carole was on a natural high from a rush of adrenalin like the cliff divers they'd been watching earlier. She decided this was a good sign, desperate to know the ins and outs of the conversation with Carlos. It would have to wait, however. She also realised her breathable clothes were struggling for air like she was. They were clinging to her sticky skin, and her hair was plastered on her face. A cool shower was what the Doctor ordered. As Carole hurried off to throw herself under hers, Maureen took charge of the situation.

'Listen, lads, I know I speak for Carole, too. We're terrible sorry like for worrying you both but her phone call was a family emergency. No, panic's over, Niall.' She held up a hand, seeing him spin in the direction Carole had gone, ready to chase after her. 'She's got it all sorted out now. And sure, the main thing is we made it back on board.'

'By the skin of your teeth,' Donal said, seemingly unwilling to let the matter drop.

'But we *did* make it back, and I think you two deserve to relax on the Lido deck and have a cocktail for your troubles. I'll go and tidy myself up.' She laid a placating hand on Donal's forearm. 'Give me half an hour.'

'I'm not letting you out of my sight, Mo,' Donal stated.

'I promise I won't disappear on you. G'won with you both, and I'll have one of those lovely Blue Lagoons while you're at it.' She could almost taste it.

Maureen was inserting her cabin key in the door, eager to get her sweaty clothes off, and she was already visualising standing beneath jets of tepid water when a voice called her name.

She looked toward its source and saw a puffy-eyed Tomasina peering around her cabin door, beckoning frantically to her.

'Maureen! I have been waiting for you to return to the ship for hours. I must speak with you!' she called out, looking decidedly unlike her glamorous stage persona in civvies.

Was she in trouble with Tomasina now, too? Maureen thought. Word spread fast on a ship and, removing the room key, she sighed. Her shower would have to be put on hold for a few minutes while she went to see what had rattled the young Polish woman. 'Is everything alright?' she asked, reaching her and seeing by her distressed demeanour that everything was not.

Tomasina broke into noisy sobs but Maureen, who was well-versed in the emotional outbursts of her daughters, knew precisely what was needed. A hug. She swept the young woman up in a sticky embrace and rubbed her back. Now wasn't the time for the 'Solider On' song because something had genuinely upset Tomasina. Instead, this called for her soothing mammy voice. 'There, there, Tomasina. Things never seem so bad once you share them. What is it that has you all upset?'

'It's my little brother, Piotr.' Tomasina sniffed into Maureen's shoulder.

Maureen recalled the first conversation she'd had with Tomasina. Piotr, pronounced as 'Peter' in her head, had gone to Dublin for work. She'd said he was naïve, and she was worried about how he'd fare away from home. Maureen felt a pinprick of fear. 'Has something happened to him?'

Tomasina sniffed louder this time. 'Yes. No. I don't know!'

Over the younger woman's dark head, Maureen saw a face peering through Niall, John, and Davey's door. The hangdog features belonged to Kevin, the comedian, and Maureen flapped her hand in his direction to signal there was nothing to worry about. Then, deciding this wasn't a conversation for

CHAPTER 24   173

public consumption, she suggested they go inside Tomasina's cabin to continue it privately.

There was no sign of Pawel, and the cabin was a mirror image of the one Maureen shared with Donal, only messier. An unfamiliar aftershave mingled with the damp smell of towels. Maureen sank into the chair by the dressing table, leaving Tomasina to perch on the edge of the bed. Her head fell into her hands as Maureen probed again. 'What's happened to get you all worked up like so?'

Tomasina raised her head, fixing red-rimmed eyes on her, and spoke up in her halting but good English. 'I phone my brother like I always do, from Mazatlán; he knows to expect my call.'

Maureen nodded, encouraging her to carry on, thinking this young man was lucky to have a sister who'd taken him under her wing like so.

'As soon as he answers, Maureen, I can hear something is wrong in his voice, but when I ask him about this he says everything is good. I don't believe him but he says the same thing he always says.' She mimicked her brother's voice, 'Everything is fine, Tomasina. Stop worrying about me. You are worse than Mama.' Her voice broke, and Maureen pulled a handful of tissues from the box on the dressing table and passed them to her. Once she'd blown her nose and mustered her emotions, she continued, 'So I telephone Mama and ask if he has contacted her. No, she says, and he doesn't answer her calls. It is making her worry. We both think Piotr is in trouble. I always know in here when this is so.' Tomasina placed her hand on her heart. 'His voice when he says life in Dublin is good reminds me of when he was a little boy and, coming home from school with bruises, he begins to wet the bed at night. He tells us then he isn't getting, erm, how you say?' She punched her flat palm several times.

'Bullied,' Maureen supplied.

'Yes, that is the word. This is a lie. So you see why I know something is wrong?'

'I do. I'm the same with my children. I can tell when the girls or Patrick aren't being truthful.' It was their shifty eyes that gave the game away. Just like Tomasina's were giving her away. It was something she'd said that told her there was more to this story than Tomasina was letting on. Fair play, though: not to say whatever she was leaving out was her prerogative, and Maureen would leave it be.

Tomasina nodded. 'You are a mama too, Maureen. I knew you would understand. This is why I am desperate to speak with you. Dublin is so far away. I can't leave the ship and go to him. Mamas's health is not so good these days. She cannot travel. Will you help me?'

Maureen took hold of the younger woman's hands and squeezed them. 'Of course I will. I'll tell you what I'll do.' She relayed a simple solution: pass Piotr's contact details on to Quinn and Tom the next day when they docked in Puerto Vallarta. 'I'll ask them to check in on him. They're good lads. They'll be happy to help. If anything is wrong, they'll sort it. He won't be on his own, Tomasina.' She hoped Piotr wasn't involved with the underworld. Perhaps he'd got mixed up with the Polish mafia if such a group existed in Dublin's fair city. She bit her bottom lip, hoping she wouldn't endanger her sons-in-law. It was too late now, though. She'd volunteered their services.

Tomasina's eyes lost their hunted look, and her shoulders slumped, but she must have read what was on Maureen's mind. 'Thank you. I promise you, he is a good boy. He won't bring trouble to your family's doorstep.'

Maureen heard the words but her eyes had wandered past Tomasina to the small table beside the couple's bed. It was cluttered with a lipstick-stained mug and a stack of books, but the framed photograph had seized her attention. A woman, Tomasina, tenderly cradled a swaddled baby. The penny dropped. The feeling in her heart Tomasina had mentioned was her mother's intuition. Maureen knew it intimately.

'He's not your brother, Tomasina, is he?'

'Why do you ask this? You think I lie to you?' Tomasina averted her gaze to the crumpled tissues in her hand, and her lashes cast shadows on her cheeks.

Maureen said nothing and, after a long second, Tomasina raised her chin to look Maureen squarely in the eye. 'I never tell anyone this.'

'Piotr's your son, isn't he?'

Tomasina nodded.

Chapter 25

♥

Tomasina

Tomasina sat at the table in the small but functional kitchen of the home she shared with her mama and Klusek, the cat, in the apartment bloki on the edge of town. The black cat was curled up where the late afternoon sun reached the armchair, oblivious to Tomasina's increasing anxiety. She was supposed to be stuffing the cabbage leaves with mince for their evening meal, which Mama would barely touch, but her hands were clasped tightly under the table. Golabki was her favourite dinner, but she knew it would taste like cardboard tonight. Her mama's back was to her at the stove, unaware of her daughter's inner turmoil as she stirred the tomato sauce.

Tomasina considered abandoning her task and scooping up Klusek, whose name meant Dumpling. She was the only one he'd tolerate cuddling him, but she stayed where she was, feeling her nails making indents in her palms, unsure how to find the strength to say what she had to. Klusek. She rolled his name in her head as an excuse not to think about what she must tell her mama. It wasn't her who'd named him. She'd have given him something more befitting his haughty demeanour if she had. Something like Antek, perhaps. It was short for Antonio, but not Leon. Never Leon.

Klusek had come to them when Mrs Dąbrowski, who'd lived at the end of the hall, had died. Her son, in his well-cut suit, had knocked on all the fourth-floor resident's doors asking if they'd take the cat in because he had a terrible allergy to pet dander and couldn't take him home. Tomasina didn't believe this for one minute. He'd barely left the big city where he lived to come to visit his mama over the years and struck her as too selfish to care for an animal. Poor Klusek, she'd thought, worried about his fate if no one agreed to give him a new home. Her pleas to be allowed the cat had been met with resistance but, in the end, her parents said he could stay so long as she fed him and emptied his litter tray. He'd also need to earn his keep and see off the mice that plagued their apartment when the weather began to cool.

She'd kept her end of the bargain. Klusek had not. Neither had her father, her tatús. He'd told her he would always be there for her and Mama then he'd died.

Tomasina could hear Mrs Joswiak tormenting her family through the paper-thin wall as she sang along to the radio while cooking as she did each evening. The woman was a terrible singer, something her tight unit of three – mama, tatús and herself – used to laugh about. Their building was old, but it had no charm and was full of secrets or so Tomasina thought. It harked back to the days not spoken about by the older folk still living here. A time when the country was under the influence of the Soviet Union and had become a communist state dictated to by Moscow.

When Tomasina tried to imagine those years, she could only see them in shades of grey like the buildings framing her town left behind to crumble as a reminder. This here, however, was her home. She knew no different. And, while it was plain and filled with hand-me-downs, it had also once been filled with life. Now, the colour was gone. Her beloved tatús had dropped dead outside the factory where he worked a few months earlier and sucked the oxygen from their apartment in his absence. Her mama told her he'd had a heart attack like his own father before him. Tomasina blamed the factory, not a congenital condition. He'd followed in his father's footsteps right through those factory gates upon leaving school, where he toiled six days a week. So, no, it wasn't a pre-existing condition but rather the back-breaking, mind-numbing work that had made her tatús' heart give up.

As she tossed the handful of soil onto his casket the day they buried him, she'd promised herself, once of age, she'd leave their town. In the moments before the earth swallowed him up, she whispered, 'I'll find a better way of life, Tatús, and I will look after Mama for you.'

How was she to keep her promise now? She'd ruined everything by giving in to Leon instead of keeping her legs crossed. She'd wanted to feel loved, though, if only for a few precious moments, and Mama was so tightly wrapped in her own grief that she didn't seem to see Tomasina these days. She would see her in a few moments, she thought, taking a deep breath and finding her voice.

'Mama, I'm pregnant.'

Chapter 26

'You must understand, Maureen,' Tomasina's dark eyes flashed, returning to the present as she focussed on her confidante, 'a pregnancy like mine twenty years ago was scandalous where we lived. Our town was small, like a big village, and people would talk. Mama and I would have been treated badly.' She shook her head, trying to convey how awful this would have been.

Maureen understood right enough. Sure, look at her own country's past. The Church and people's attitudes may have grown lenient in recent years. However, the memories of the Catholic institution and its faithful's harsh and unforgiving treatment were scored into the psyche of those who'd suffered. Hadn't she worried about Moira's unplanned pregnancy, and she'd been a grown woman of twenty-six? Oh-ho, yes. She'd been more shaken by the news than the Pope's hand, and there'd been none of the calming pranayama breathing on her part; it had been Darth Vader all the way when her daughter conveyed the news. After reaching for the wine bottle in the fridge, her first instinct was to demand Tom make an honest woman of her daughter. She'd been terrified about how Moira, her fragile daughter with the biggest mouth in Dublin's uppermost south, would cope. Kiera had been the making of her and Tom. Babbies were a blessing, but if she'd come to her as a teenager . . .

'Leon, the father, he was a boy himself. He'd had his way but wouldn't want to pay the consequences. Mama told me if my tatús were alive, he would drag me around to the boy's house and insist Leon do the honourable thing. But I know Leon. He will call me a bad thing and deny being the father. His parents would shut the door in her face, and we would be shamed. I told Mama this, and she began to cry. So many tears. I didn't know what to do because I couldn't make it better.' Tomasina shrugged.

Maureen already had an image of a woman made thin by grief, probably only a few years older than Tomasina was now, firmly in her mind. She pictured her eyes haunted with deep loss, round with shock at her daughter's announcement. Her hands clasped in prayer before hunching over, sobbing, and leaving the sauce bubbling in the pot to dry up. The poor woman would have wondered what she'd done to deserve losing her husband and having to face dealing with their teenage daughter's pregnancy alone.

'Things worked out in the end, though,' Maureen said, trying to inject a note of cheerfulness into the maudlin atmosphere. 'Didn't they?'

Tomasina was lost in her painful memories, however. 'Mama went to bed eventually, and so did I. The next day, she says Piotr came to her at night and told her what we must do.'

Now, Maureen was lost. 'Your mammy had a vision of your unborn son?'

'No, my tatús, he visited her. My father's name was Piotr, too. Mama says she hears his voice as if he is standing in the room with her, and he tells her that this baby is a gift and that she should raise the child on her own. The baby will be my brother or sister.'

It wouldn't be the first time this subterfuge had taken place, Maureen thought. Sure, in the village of Ballyclegg where she'd grown up, it was common knowledge Maggie Connor's son, Mick, was her grandson and his older sister, who called in from London on auspicious occasions like birthdays or Christmas, was his mam. Everybody had guessed as much except poor Mick. Still, ignorance was bliss, she supposed.

'Mama begins telling people that Piotr has left her a wonderful gift. A baby. So many years, they try for another child. "It is a miracle," she says.' Tomasina raised her eyes to the ceiling as she said 'miracle'.

Maureen kept to herself the sentiment of being able to convince yourself of anything if you say it often enough. 'And you were happy to go along with all of this?'

Tomasina shrugged. 'The lie had been told. I had no other choice. Besides, I think it is a miracle. A miracle to see my mama eating once more and the colour it comes back to her cheeks.' Tomasina's hands went to her own cheeks. 'It was the best thing for the baby and for Mama.'

And the hardest thing for this poor girl, Maureen thought, wondering over the lengths people would go to to hold their heads up in their community.

'As the months pass and I begin to get bigger, we are lucky because it is winter. I hide my bulk under my coat, and Mama pads her middle with cushions. I cannot make a noise when the pains come because our walls are so thin. Mama has read books on what to do when the baby is ready and helps me deliver my baby, a boy. My Piotr. She says the birth is an easy one.' Tomasina's grimace said she wasn't convinced of this. 'When I hold him, I feel so much love. You are a mama. You know this feeling.'

Maureen did; she remembered being overwhelmed with it once she'd got over having given birth to pumpkin-headed babies.

'Then I hand my boy to my mama. I never regret him. He brought the colour back into our lives and he is loved.'

'Does Pawel know any of this?'

Tomasina shook her head hard. 'No. I have never told anyone until now. And, Maureen, he must never know. I have already broken my promise to my mama telling you.' The younger woman studied her face imploringly.

'Yours is not my story to tell, Tomasina.' Maureen would not breathe a word. 'How did you meet Pawel?' She'd heard this much of the Polish woman's story and wanted to know the rest.

The sadness cloaking Tomasina lifted and she smiled. 'Piotr is six years old the day I first see Pawel, and my son knows me as his sister. It's not easy for me in this situation. I'm still young and a little naïve. Sometimes, I badly want to tell him the truth. I know this is selfish, though. Pawel is working on a building site near our apartment bloki. He is so handsome with big muscles,' she flexed her bicep to demonstrate, 'and it is love at first sight for both of us.'

Maureen smiled at this.

'You are smiling. I, too, believe this is a myth until it happens to me. Within six months, we were married. Pawel wants us to move to the city so he can follow his dream of being an illusionist and travelling the world. He has wanted this since he was as small as Piotr, and his parents took him to a magic show. He is a determined boy who studied his craft, practised hard, and performed the tricks even though people tell him it is a crazy job. I agree to move away because I think it will be easier than staying. It hurts to be on the outside looking in, and Mama and I have fought a lot since Piotr was born.'

Maureen could guess the rest of the journey that had seen Tomasina become part of the Dreamweaver illusionist act that brought the couple here to the *Mayan Princess* eventually. However, she found it hard to believe that Pawel hadn't figured out the truth of Piotr's parentage. It was plain to see. Perhaps he had and thought it best to let things lie.

'Sometimes Pawel gets annoyed at how protective I am over Piotr. He says, "He's your brother, not your child. He's your mama's responsibility." It is, what is the word?'

'Ironic.'

'Yes, it is an ironic thing to say, no?'

Maureen nodded although, personally, she just thought it sad.

The door to the cabin opened then, and the two women swung guiltily toward Pawel. He had a towel draped around his neck and proper gym gear on, not the multi-purpose shorts Donal had opted for. If he was surprised to see his wife with red-rimmed eyes and Maureen sitting in his cabin, his expression didn't show it as he greeted her. 'I hear you only just make it back on the ship?'

Maureen was about to reply when she heard her name shouted frantically in the corridor. 'What an earth? Excuse me, Pawel!' She pushed past the Polish man glistening with sweat to see Donal marauding past. A panther patrolling the corridor. In his hand was her key tag.

'Donal, what are you shouting about? I'm here. I've been having a girl's chat with Tomasina.'

'Oh, that's just great, Mo. While you've been in there,' he jabbed manically at Tomasina and Pawel's cabin, 'I've lost another ten years off my life expectancy. That's twenty years gone in the space of a few hours.'

'Hold that thought, Donal.' Maureen ducked back into the cabin. 'Tomasina, I promise I'll get Quinn and Tom to check in on Piotr.' Her reward was a grateful smile and, leaving her to explain what she meant to Pawel, Maureen closed the door on the couple. 'C'mere to me now, Donal McCarthy, you great big eejit. What did you think had happened to me?'

'Alien abduction,' Donal said weakly, only half-joking as the chords in his neck slowly returned to their standard size. 'I was on a knife's edge, Mo, after this afternoon's shenanigans with you and Carole nearly being left behind in Matzalán. You said you'd be half an hour tops, a quick shower, you said. When Niall decided you weren't coming up on deck and polished off your Blue Lagoon, I panicked and raced downstairs to find you. When I reached our cabin, the door was ajar, the key in the slot, and there was no sign of you. I immediately catastrophised the situation and went to rescue you.'

'Well, thank you, my hero, but as you can see, I'm grand and sorry I worried you.' She gave him a squeeze because it was nice to be loved. Then, linking her arm through his, led him back to their cabin. 'It's been quite the afternoon, alright. What with Carole and her family issue. Then Tomasina needing a shoulder to cry on because she's worried about her younger brother.' She brought Donal up to speed with her plan to pass on Piotr's details to Quinn and Tom so they could check in on him and hopefully put Tomasina's mind at ease.

Donal was almost as zen as Maureen after a yoga class by the time he kicked the cabin door closed with his heel. He clasped Maureen by her shoulders and planted a kiss on her forehead. 'You're one in a million, Mo. I'm a lucky man. You've a special way with people. You could have been a therapist in another life the way they open up around you.'

Maureen smiled. 'It's me who's a lucky woman, Donal. And it comes from years of running a guesthouse. Everybody has a story to tell, and something about temporarily staying somewhere sees people wanting to share what they're holding here.' She placed her hand on her heart. 'I don't think it's much different aboard a cruise ship.' Nevertheless, she added 'Therapist' beneath 'Motivational Speaker' under her growing list of talents.

Chapter 27

♥

Maureen wrapped the pink scarf, doubling as a pashmina bought on her Greek holiday, around her shoulders and made to curl up on the lounger. The silver lamé gown wasn't made for curling up, however, so she sat with her legs out straight and fiddled with the back of the seat until she had it just so. She'd a cup of tea on the deck alongside her in easy reach and a plate of cheese and crackers. It was all that was on offer in the buffet this time of night. The moon in the starlit sky resembled a giant pumpkin, making her feel philosophical as she gazed at it. The longer she stared, the more she fancied she could see Patrick as a babby's face in it. Sure, it was like the start of the *Teletubbies* programme, but instead of the babby's face in the sun, giggling, it was a moonfaced Pat. Movement out the corner of her eye saw her drag her attention from the full moon to where Carole was approaching her. She must have come straight from the Atrium as she'd slipped her heels off, dangling them from one hand while carrying a cup of tea. Maureen gave her a wave.

There'd been no chance for the two women to catch up earlier, not because of a lack of trying. Carole had tapped on Maureen and Donal's cabin door when she'd had a dinner break, a window between her evening and afternoon sets. However, the couple, shattered from the day's events, had dozed off and had not heard her knock. So, it had fallen to Maureen to make a hasty arrangement to meet on the Lido deck at 11pm as she passed through the Atrium to the Havana Lounge for The Gamblers' performance.

The show tonight had been great fun, with the audience getting into the swing of things on the dancefloor. Yet, Maureen had been counting down the songs until their encore performance of "Coward of the County". She'd been desperate for 11pm to roll around to hear how Carole's phone call with Carlos had gone. Donal stepped away from the mic when the final notes were sung, and Maureen assured him not to worry, saying, 'I'll meet you back in the cabin later.' Then, leaving him and the lads to mix and mingle with the passengers who'd come to see them play, she hurried up to the Lido deck.

'How was the show?' Carole asked, settling down on the lounger next to Maureen and being careful not to slosh her tea.

Maureen thought she looked stylish in her black blazer worn over a pale blue trouser suit and told her so before replying. 'The show went over very well, especially "The Gambler". We always start with it. However, there was an unfortunate incident with a fella who skidded over due to his haste to hit the dance floor. We think he slipped a disc. His cowboy boots had no grip on the soles.' She tutted.

Carole made a suitably sympathetic noise. 'I'm looking forward to seeing The Gamblers at the Haybales and Hoedown party the night after next. My set's finishing an hour earlier because most people will be at the party. It will be my first opportunity to see Niall playing guitar and you all doing your thing. I can't wait to learn to line dance.'

'Well, just be sure to wear the grippy cowboy boots. And at least your schedules have given you and Niall plenty of free time together during the day,' Maureen waggled her eyebrows suggestively, making the other woman laugh.

CHAPTER 27

'Subtle, you are not, Maureen. Although, I won't deny I'm enjoying getting to know Niall.'

Maureen made a note to herself to tell Niall to do the Eric Clapton thing with his face, where he made the audience feel like his guitar was talking, at the Haybale and Hoedown party. Personally speaking, Maureen thought Niall looked like he needed an enema when he screwed his face up with the emotion of his solo like so, but the audience loved it. Chances were, Carole would too. 'And how was your performance tonight?' Maureen asked, blowing on her tea.

'Good, thanks.' Then Carole grinned, copying Maureen as she said, 'Although there was an unfortunate incident whereby a woman, three sheets to the wind on cocktails, trailed toilet paper stuck to her shoe all the way from the Ladies' to the Atrium to request I play "Piano Man".'

'No! She'll be mortified in the morning.'

'Or too hungover to care.'

Both women shared a sanctimonious tea-sipping moment before Maureen reached for the plate. 'Cheese and biscuit?'

'Don't mind if I do.'

Once Carole had placed a chunk of cheddar on her cracker, Maureen got to the point of their late-night rendezvous. 'So, c'mon, tell me. How did your conversation with Carlos go?' Annoyingly, Carole popped the cheese and cracker in her mouth and was as slow as a cow chewing cud, drawing out the moment's drama. It would seem the moon was in on the act, too, because it chose that moment to hide behind a cloud and, while it didn't plunge them into darkness, it was like the lights going down at the cinema.

'Sorry,' Carole said finally, with a grin that said she was anything but as she brushed the crumbs off her blazer.

Maureen stashed the plate out of reach. 'You're not having another until you've answered my question.'

'Okay, I don't want to jinx things, but the call went well. Carlos heard me out. He let me speak without interrupting, and he was gracious in accepting my apology. He said he'd like to move forward and that I should be a part of his, Emma's, and Charlotte's lives. He promised he'll talk to Emma for me.'

'Oh, Carole, I'm delighted, so I am!' Maureen gave a little clap.

Carole was beaming from ear to ear but, still, she erred on the side of caution. 'I hope Emma will listen to what Carlos has to pass on. She can hold a grudge.' The grin faded. 'I want her to accept my apology and understand I realise how misguided my actions were but know they did come from a place of love.' She wrung her hands. 'I'm going to be so on edge each time we're in port and I check my emails.'

'You'll hear from her.' Maureen could feel it in her water. 'And what did you make of Carlos?'

'Once I'd finished laying it all bare for him and he had a chance to talk, I got the impression that he's a solid young man. I liked him. I wish I'd given him a chance instead of seeing him as a threat.' Carole's voice grew thick. 'Oh, Maureen, I've wasted so much time. What a fool I've been.'

'Now that's enough of that. No more looking back, Carole. What's done is done, and you can't change things. It's what happens next that matters.'

Carole's eyes glistened in the semi-darkness. 'You're right. There's power in positive thinking, right?'

'Right so, shall we drink to the future?' Maureen reached for her mug and raised it. Carole did the same, and Maureen recited, 'Always remember to forget the troubles that passed away, but never forget to remember the blessings that come each day. Cheers.'

'Cheers.' They tapped their mugs together. 'Is that an Irish toast?' Carole asked, once she'd had a sip of her tea.

'It is. We've loads. You name an occasion, we Irish have got it covered.'

'Not just the Irish. I've one we're fond of in Oz for you, too. It's very profound.'

'Oh yes?'

'Yes. Ready?'

'Ready, but hurry up, Carole, because my tea's getting cold.'

'Here we go . . . Cheers, big ears!'

The two women were still laughing when the moon came out from behind the cloud five minutes later.

Chapter 28

Maureen slept through the Sunrise Yoga session for the second time that week. Still, she managed to be on the top deck for the *Mayan Princess*'s 8am arrival into the balmy bay of Banderas in Puerto Vallarta. Donal, who'd also slept through going to the gym accidentally on purpose, had announced he was a new man as he strode without a hint of the bandy legs down the corridor outside their cabin to the lift. From their vantage point, Maureen and Donal soaked up the view of the city set amongst lush, tropical scenery. All the while Davey, who'd trailed up the stairs after them, gave them a monotone monologue from his guidebook as to what was what.

'And see the church with the crown perched on top of the spire? That's Our Lady of Guadalupe.'

Maureen lifted her sunglasses and followed the direction of Davey's outstretched arm to where his finger was pointing. 'It's spectacular,' she breathed, admiring the spire that looked like a royal crown had been placed on top of it. She'd be sure to light candles for Carole and Tomasina's Piotr when they visited it.

Davey looked pleased, as though he was responsible for the place of worship. He began jabbering about how it took 84 years to go from a rustic little chapel to the magnificent landmark structure they could see before them. Maureen cut him off as the boat navigated into its berth in the city's modern cruise port and led the charge to gather the troops for a quick breakfast. There was no time for lingering over a second cup of tea or coffee today, not if they wanted to enjoy a full day exploring. So as soon as knives, forks, spoons, and cups were set down, they donned hats and slapped on sun cream, ready for disembarkation.

Maureen avoided eye contact with the security officers as they were swept off the boat in the tide of sunburned passengers; she supposed Carole would be doing the same, knowing they'd be sure to be back at the ship in good time this afternoon. Today, the group bypassed the colourful craft stalls and merely waved at the exuberant Mariachi band as they exited the terminal to be greeted by a crowd of touts eager to sell their tours and whisk them away on a whirlwind adventure.

'Look at that,' Maureen said, her attention caught by a pistol-wielding pirate statue. It was a world away from the bronze Molly Malone figure on Grafton Street, also known as the 'Tart with the Cart'. 'Will you take my photograph next to it?' Maureen thrust the camera at Donal and moved next to the statue to strike a pose. She raised her chin so there wasn't a whiff of the second one that had taken up residence like an unwelcome squatter. Then she thrust a flowy trouser leg forward, angling her hip in a slimming angle like the celebs in magazines did.

'Say cheese.' Donal raised the camera.

Maureen opened her mouth to say cheese but, as she did, the statue suddenly mimicked her pose, and a scream burst from her lips instead. 'It's alive!'

The statue resumed its former pose like they'd imagined the whole thing. Donal and the others were bent double as they all put their hands in their pockets to toss loose change the street performer's way. Maureen wasn't amused but, sure, it would have been a shot for the album if the statue person hadn't moved. Now captured on film forevermore was a slender pirate statue with a firm jawline and a female Jack in the Box with her gob hanging open. She moved a few steps away, searching in her bag for her sunglasses, aware a hot debate had been entered over who fancied doing what.

'I need to send an urgent email home before we do anything,' Maureen called over to where John had turned away from the others and was negotiating with a cowboy hat, blue jean-wearing tout who came up to his chest. She gave up on her sunglasses, deciding she'd just have to buy a make-do cheap pair, and sidled over to Carole, keeping a wary eye on the pirate statue.

'The men want to do a Tequilla tasting tour at a local distillery,' Carole informed her.

Davey, leaving John to fix his fair price, said to the two women, 'Purely for cultural enriching purposes, ladies. It's Mexico's national drink, after all.'

Maureen and Carole eyed one another sceptically, and Maureen spoke up, 'If you say so, Davey. Before we go anywhere, though, Carole and I have to call in at an internet café. We've important business. Did you catch that, John?'

'I did Maureen, important business.' A few seconds later, John shook hands with the tout who flashed his gold tooth at them, tipped his hat, then, hooking his thumbs in his jeans belt loops, introduced himself as Francisco.

'But you, my friends, can call me Pancho. I look forward to showing you around my family farm, left to my brother and me by our beloved mama and papa. At the López farm, you will learn how Mexico's finest tequila is made.'

'Yes, but will we get to taste it?' Davey butted in.

'Yes, my friend, you can taste-test our many varieties and purchase directly from the manufacturers. Myself and my brother.'

CHAPTER 28

The lads began working out how many bottles they could sneak back on the boat.

Pancho's mobile phone, attached to his jeans by a leather pouch, rang. He ignored it, saying over the ringing that he would meet them in one hour outside the Church of our Lady of Guadalupe. Then, using his hand to demonstrate hanging a left off the Malécon followed by a right, he began waggling his middle and index fingers to demonstrate walking in a straight line for a few metres, telling them where they could use the internet. 'See you in one *hora*.' He swaggered over to a line of white minivans.

Pancho's helpful directions saw Maureen sitting in front of a winking computer monitor five minutes later. She was patting around her person, trying to locate her glasses, when she saw Donal at the café window. He tapped the top of his head and she, reaching up, found that's where her glasses were perched. 'What would I do without you?' she mouthed, slipping them on and logging into her Hotmail account. It would be best to send the email straight to O'Mara's inbox, she decided, knowing Bronagh would ensure it made it into the right people's hands and, entering the address, she moved down to the subject line to type 'URGENT MATTER FOR TOM AND QUINN TO ATTEND TO'.

Carole was sitting directly opposite her, and Maureen could feel waves of dejection coming from her. She'd slumped in her chair and there was no need to stretch her neck and look over the computer to see the other woman's face. She knew it would be long. Emma hadn't yet accepted the olive branch her mother had held out.

'Give her a chance to digest what Carlos passed on, Carole,' Maureen said, digging out the piece of paper Tomasina must have slid under their cabin door first thing that morning with Piotr's contact details in Dublin.

'It's going to be a rollercoaster of emotions whenever I check my Hotmail account from now on, I expect,' Carole said dully, her gaze turning to the window through which she could see the lads milling about on the pavement outside. 'I'll wait out there for you, Maureen.'

Maureen nearly said, 'Soldier on,' but decided on, 'Chin up' instead. 'It's bound to be an emotional wait, Carole, but remember it's been less than 24 hours.'

'I know. Give me a few minutes to wallow then I'll put it into perspective.' Carole mustered up a smile as she left Maureen typing away. Once she'd finished, she scanned over her words satisfied that she had conveyed the need for speed in doing a welfare check on the young Pole. Sure, he didn't live far from the guesthouse. They could run round to his flat as part of their marathon training if they wanted, she thought, pushing 'send'. She paid up and exited the café, instantly feeling the humidity press down on her like someone had tossed a wet blanket over her head. 'Shall we pay a visit to the church, then?'

'Better now than after the tequila tour.' Niall did that chortling thing Donal was prone to.

Maureen put her glasses away in their case, then remembered she'd tried and failed to locate her sunglasses. 'I forgot my sunglasses and it's terrible glary out here. Have we got time for me to pick up a pair on the way?'

'There's no need, Mo, they're hooked into your shirt.' Donal pointed to the neckline of her top.

Maureen looked down, and there they were. Her sunglasses. She really would be lost without Donal!

Chapter 29

♥

Pancho kept his word, and the group found him loitering outside the Church of our Lady of Guadalupe, where Maureen had lit her candles for Piotr and Carole precisely one hour later.

'I am parked around the corner; follow me,' he instructed with a glint of gold tooth before setting off briskly. The party of five Irish tourists and one Australian struggled to keep up thanks to the humidity, making it feel like they were wading through water. At last, though, they reached the mini-van after being led down a network of dark, narrow lanes.

It was a rumpty old thing with dents in the side and arid soil embedded in the paintwork; Maureen noticed as Davey announced, 'I'm in the front because I'm the biggest.' He clambered in while Pancho, after a few attempts, managed to slide the passenger door across and usher them all inside. Once comfortably seated, he slammed the door. Maureen turned back to Carole; they exchanged glances over what they'd let themselves in for.

'Cash up front,' Pancho said, hopping behind the van wheel and twisting around to give them all a glimpse of that gold tooth again.

'Cash is king, eh Pancho?' Donal chortled, digging around his pocket for his wallet.

'I've got this,' Niall said to Carole.

'That's very generous of you, Niall. Cheers pal.' John leaned forward in his seat and patted his bandmate on the shoulder.

'Not you, you eejit: Carole.'

American dollars exchanged hands, and Maureen kept her thoughts on John needing to switch his choice of deodorant up to extra strength to cope with the Mexican humidity to herself.

Pancho turned the key and the van rumbled to life, sending a blast of frigid air into the stuffy back.

'That's a blessed relief,' Maureen said, wafting her top and enjoying the air con.

The van nosed away from the kerb, and Pancho easily navigated the narrow lanes until they emerged onto a busy main road. That's when a peculiar phenomenon was noticed. It was Donal who pointed it out.

'Why are there so many pea-green Volkswagen Beetles on the road, Pancho?' He asked the question on everyone's lips because every second vehicle was a V-dub zipping along. It was a sight that felt like a mass hallucination.

'They're taxis, my friends,' Pancho spoke up. 'They are cheap to run, and it is easy to take the front seat out to make room in the back for passengers.'

That made sense, Maureen thought, glad she wasn't seeing things. 'I've some trivia for you, Pancho. The first Volkswagen Beetle to be assembled outside of Germany was in Dublin.'

Pancho laughed. 'You have taught me something.'

Maureen puffed up, pleased, and they all ignored the sudden backfiring of the mini-van.

It didn't take long to leave the urban buildings behind, and soon they were teaching Pancho something else: the song, 'It's a Long Way to Tipperary'. The van bumped along roads with fields filled with spiky teal plants on either side as they sang their hearts out.

CHAPTER 29   197

'This is what we farm,' Pancho interrupted the song. 'The agave plant is used to make the tequila.'

'Who'd have thought, Mo?' Donal said, gazing out the window as Pancho turned the steering wheel left, and they began bouncing down a long dirt drive where a low-slung series of buildings forming the López ranch was visible ahead. He pulled up outside an open area closer to the barn buildings than the red-tiled roof house and, as Pancho wrenched the handbrake up, a man emerged through the clouds of dust. Maureen half-expected to see Clint Eastwood standing there, eyes twitching, hand at the ready by his gun like in his Spaghetti Western days. She was also beginning to feel panicked by Pancho's third failed attempt to open the passenger door. At last, however, he wrenched it open, and she all but fell out behind Donal to stand blinking in the vast open space.

A bar area with shade cover and a row of stools lined up in front of it waited for them and, next to that, a barn in which barrels were housed. They were rolled on each other, stacked high, and filling the cavernous space was a vat and other complicated brewing machinery. She thought the distillery was a mix of old and new, taking in the enormous brick oven and stone wheel from what seemed like the Dark Ages. Their host was talking, and she focused her attention on him.

'Welcome to Lopéz Farm. I am Enriqué, Pancho's older and wiser brother.'

Pancho pulled a comical face, making them laugh.

'He could be Pancho's twin,' she whispered to Donal. 'Right down to the gold tooth.'

'Only he's a good head taller,' Donal whispered back, shaking Enriqué's hand.

Maureen was glad she'd brought a big bottle of water with her. Rather than head straight to the bar, Enriqué was swift to get their tour underway by leading them across to the nearby fields of agave plants they'd seen from the van. She was also glad of her hat as she took a long swig before passing the bottle to Donal and reminding him of the importance of keeping hydrated. Her thoughts turned fleetingly toward the elusive *Mayan Princess* drink bottle. Not wanting to ruin an enjoyable day, she tuned into what turned out to be the fascinating process of harvesting the agave plant to make tequila.

Enriqué informed them as they clustered around him that it took six to ten years for the agave to mature, before the farmers sliced the spiked leaves away with a tool called a *coa* to reveal the pineapple-like core. 'Authentic tequila must be made with 51 percent or more of the agave sugar. Ours here at López Farm is premium. We use one hundred percent. Impressed nods went around the group, and the word 'premium' was tossed about. Enriqué gestured for them to follow him over to the shade of the barn and, more than happy to escape the harsh glare of an unforgiving sun, they did so. Here, they were shown how the core, or pina, was chopped into pieces and baked in the brick oven, which Maureen had noticed earlier. Heads tilted to one side as he explained the process left them with fermentable sugars.

'How on earth did people figure out these things in the first place?' Carole whispered to Maureen.

'It should be the eighth holy mystery, alright, Carole.' She was pleased her friend had shaken off her fug and was absorbed in what they were being shown.

'Here's one I prepared earlier,' Enriqué announced with the aplomb of a television chef, making them laugh.

He was a good host and teacher, Maureen thought as he demonstrated how the big stone wheel called a tahona was used to crush the baked pina to release aguamiel. 'In English, this means honey water.'

'Nectar of the Gods, eh Enriqué?' John chortled, and Maureen caught Carole rolling her eyes and smiled.

The complicated fermentation process and distillation followed, and all of these things had gone over Maureen's head. She was glad when Enriqué led them to the bar where Pancho had lined up shot glasses. The lads were gagging for a sample. Carole confided to Maureen that she'd once had a rather wild night in her student days on the tequila and had suffered terribly the next day, so she would be going easy on the sampling.

'I'm with you,' Maureen replied, plonking on her stool, her feet automatically tapping to the music emanating from the American jukebox set up in the corner of the bar.

Pancho clapped his hands, rubbing them together. 'This afternoon, we will be sampling López Farm's finest tequila.' He gestured to the bottles with their colourful labels on the laden shelf behind him. 'We have a selection of Blanco, which means it is un-aged tequila; Reposado, which has aged in the barrels for two months to a year; Añejo, which matures for a minimum of one to three years; and finally, Extra Añejo. This is my personal favourite, as good things take time. This must remain in the barrel for three years, during which time it takes on the oaky flavour of the timber. We'll start with the Blanco.' He fetched a bottle, opened it, and sloshed the clear liquid into the shot glasses, but when he reached Maureen's, he saw she'd placed her hand over the glass.

'I don't have a strong constitution for the hard stuff, Pancho, so just a wee one for me.'

'Maureen, it's a shot glass; you can't get any smaller.' John peered around Davey.

Maureen eyed Carole's full glass. 'We'll see how we go then.' She took her hand away and, once Pancho had recapped the bottle and put it back on the shelf, she raised it.

'I think you will enjoy the freshness and crisp flavour. In Mexico, we say *Pa' arriba*, which means lifting your glass.' Those that hadn't done so did so. '*Pa' abajo*, lower your glass.'

'You're a big tease, so you are, Pancho,' Maureen giggled. It was definitely not a chortle.

Pancho laughed, '*Pa' centro*, point your glass to the group. Now, *Pa' dentro*! We drink.'

Things got a little hazy for Maureen after her second taste test of the agreeable Reposado. One minute, she was sampling the liquor that no longer burned on the way down at the bar. The next, she demanded that Pancho put the Champs classic "Tequila" song on the jukebox. As the party song blared, she kicked her legs to the left and right, attempting to get a conga party line dancing around the dusty yard. There was a vague snapshot of bumping back down that long dirt driveway, followed by a big blank. Then she was back on the ship and standing under a cold shower, swearing she would never touch tequila again. 'It's touched by the divil, the tequila, so it is, Donal,' she declared.

Later that night...

It wasn't easy performing with a banging head, Maureen thought. She'd sobered up in the hours since boarding the ship, showering and having something to eat while muttering about wishing she'd hydrated more. A *Mayan Princess* drink bottle would have served as a reminder to sip from it. Nevertheless, she prided herself on being a professional and her smile was plastered on her dial as she banged her tambourine. She just wished Donal wouldn't sing *quite* so loudly.

Chapter 30

♥

Day 6 - The Haybale and Hoedown Party

The ship had begun its gentle return journey along the Pacific coast toward Los Angeles. Maureen had started the second to last day on their first cruise with a yoga session. It hadn't been easy to drag herself up to the Lido deck at such a ridiculously early hour, leaving Donal snoring blissfully. Needs must, however, and penance for her tequila sins had to be paid. Besides, having arranged to meet Carole for the class, she had no choice. Halfway through, however, she was glad she'd made the effort because the sunshine and sun salutations were good for the soul.

'Tune him out, Carole,' Maureen whispered, referencing the heavy breather who was like a cheese grater on the soul before telling herself, *God loves a tri*er. And she'd tried. Throughout the class, Maureen had dropped helpful pointers on the various positions Christie guided them into. These had not been well received, with their instructor glaring at her stony-faced instead of implementing the tucking of the tailbone and what-not. In the end she'd zipped it, deciding it was better to leave their multi-tasking Director of Entertainment to Rosi to sort out when she and the rest of the family joined them for a week. She'd show Christie a thing or two on how it was done. From now on, her lips would be sealed for the duration of the sessions except for when it came to breathing in through the nose and out through the mouth. Carole, who was more a 'walk around the park' than a bendy yoga girl, said she'd enjoyed the class and felt lithe after all that lengthening of the spine.

The rest of the morning unfolded leisurely, with Maureen and Donal doing their own thing, finding a sunny position to relax poolside. At the same time, Davey, John, the redhead woman and her friend played Shuffleboard – Donal and Maureen weren't invited. Niall and Carole had discovered a mutual love of jigsaw puzzles. They were in the throes of a one thousand-piece picture puzzle in the library.

As she lay enjoying the sun's rays, Maureen noticed a tendency to begin thinking about the next meal on the ship before the last one had gone down. She'd hold her hand up to salivating over the prospect of chicken parmigiana and the rest when she had her eyes shut trying to digest the omelette, toast and pastries, enjoying doing nothing with her beloved by her side while children shrieked and splashed nearby. Not surprisingly, she and Donal let themselves down at lunchtime at the Lido Buffet by trying and failing to moderate their portion sizes. As they pushed their chairs back, Donal clutched his tummy, groaning over being full to the brim. Maureen reached for the Rennies, and they solemnly promised one another to do better on their second run down the Mexican Riviera.

'Shall we hit the Champagne Art Auction, Mo, for a free glass of bubbles?' Donal suggested as they got up from the table.

'In for a penny, in for a pound, Donal,' Maureen said, given their good intentions had evaporated over their piled-high plates.

She'd been sure to sit on her free hand throughout the fast-paced auction, fearing the bubbling volcano sensation would see her raise it and spend all their week's earnings on a print they didn't have room for on the walls back home in Howth. As it was, they left the auction the proud owners of a Warhol pop art print of a can of Campbell's soup. It had transpired Donal should have been sitting on his hand, and when Maureen asked why the soup, he replied, 'Tomato's my favourite.'

They were due to rehearse their line dancing numbers in the quiet of the Havana Lounge at 2pm for the evening's Haybale and Hoedown party with the rest of The Gamblers when Maureen caught sight of Tony the Manchild in the distance.

'Donal, I'm after having an epiphany!' Before Donal could ask what it was, Maureen was yoo-hooing the dancer-singer. This time, he didn't run away. Instead, Tony greeted her and Donal with a smile, saying he was pleased to see them.

Maureen got straight to the point. 'Tony, you'll be aware of the Haybales and Hoedown party on the Lido Deck this evening?'

'I am, Maureen. It's a highlight of the week for the passengers after the Latino Stars of the Sea show, that's always a firm fave. What about it?'

Maureen let that slide, given it was a favour she was seeking. 'Well, it occurred to me that in the costume department of the Grand Theatre there might be a costume I could borrow to look the part because I'm leading the line dancing and judging the dance-off. I'm thinking cowgirl.'

'I've always wanted to try line dancing,' Tony said with a wistfulness that saw Maureen hit with a second epiphany.

So it was later that night, under a star-dappled sky, The Gamblers had drawn a large crowd up to the Lido deck. Maureen loved the special headset mic she was wearing to call out the steps as she and her dance partner Tony led the masses through the basics of line dancing. Tony was a fast learner when he joined Maureen at rehearsals in the Havana Louge earlier and quickly picked up the moves. He was also thoroughly enjoying his headset. Nobody could say they didn't look the part either dressed in the cowgirl and cowboy costumes unearthed from the wardrobe department of the *Mayan Princess*. They had a past performance of *Annie Get Your Gun* to thank for their outfits.

Maureen knew she was in the company of kindred spirits as they quickstepped the eager passengers, who'd also dressed to look the part, through a medley of classic line-dance hits like the 'Boot Scootin Boogey', 'Cotton Eye Joe', 'Achy Breaky Heart', 'The Watermelon Crawl' and a fancy footwork take on 'The Macarena'.

The dance-off that followed was a hit with only one altercation on the dancefloor, which Maureen put down to a misinterpretation of the 'Boot Scootin Boogie' moves. Boot, not butt.

The winner who performed to Kenny Loggins' 'Footloose', which strained Donal's vocal cords and tested Maureen and Tony's line dancing abilities, took home a *Mayan Princess* water bottle.

Chapter 31

♥

Three weeks later - Port of Los Angeles

Maureen and Donal stood fidgeting from foot to foot in the foyer of the Atrium in anxious anticipation of welcoming all the family aboard the *Mayan Princess*. They'd arranged for John, Davey, Niall, and Carole to meet them on the Lido Deck for the Sail Away party. Carole was eager to be introduced to the family she'd heard so much about. A flurry of excited passengers passed by, looking about them wide-eyed, newbies to cruise ship life. Maureen wondered if they looked like that when they first stepped onboard, marvelling over how much had happened in such a short time.

Carole and Niall were like smitten teenagers and had been told to get a room more than once in the Lido Buffet. It was enough to put you off your roast pork and crackling, Davey had declared, nevertheless crunching into the pork fat with gusto. The change in Carole since Maureen's first meeting with her waiting for the lift was phenomenal. Emma had written to her a week after Carole bravely spoke to Carlos. She'd had a lightness to her step and a glow to her skin ever since. Niall could take some credit for the latter because love couldn't be bought in a bottle and slapped on the face for instant results. Maureen knew herself; love was the best potion of all. She squeezed Donal's arm.

Initially, Carole and Emma had cleared the air over the internet, graduating to heartfelt phone calls, which also involved much cooing down the phone to little Charlotte whom Carole couldn't wait to meet when her contract was up. *What would happen to her and Niall then?* Maureen wondered. Time would tell.

A hush fell over the Atrium as Captain Franco limped past, still managing to ooze 'I'm in command' importance. 'How's the ankle, Captain Franco?' Maureen asked. She strongly suspected Donal of foot-tripping Captain Franco as he masterfully strode past their table in the Lido Buffet the night before. He'd been humming 'You Should Be Dancing' at the time.

Captain Franco paused to address her. 'It is tender, but I will live. Thank you for asking.'

Maureen preened under the Captain's intense, unwavering gaze. He was masterful *and* polite.

'It was fortunate for me that the young man from the Latino Nights show was on hand to perform first aid.'

'Tony the Man— er Tony and, yes, he'd not long passed his first aid course.' Tony, who said he wasn't stalking the Captain, he just happened to be there in the Lido Buffet too, had been in his element producing a bandage like Pawel in the middle of his illusionist act. He'd deftly wrapped it around the Captain's ankle and sent him on his way before he knew what was happening.

Now, hearing Donal break into 'Stayin' Alive' as the Captain strode off, Maureen trod on his foot.

'They're not here yet?' Tomasina appeared with Pawel by her side. She had two boxes of Polish Wedel chocolates to gift Tom and Quinn as a thank you for their help with Piotr.

Quinn and Tom had tried phoning the number Maureen emailed through for the Polish lad and, not getting anywhere, had gone round to the address. Piotr had reluctantly let them into the house that reeked of damp, and they'd not liked what they'd seen or heard. Drug paraphernalia littered the kitchen worktop. Piotr had assured them that it didn't belong to him, but places to rent were scarce and pickings slim; he had to take what he could get, which wasn't much on what he was earning. It had transpired the young Pole was being taken advantage of in a busy Dublin restaurant's kitchen where he was working for cash in hand: slave wages. When Tom had enquired why he'd stayed in Dublin when things were clearly grim, he'd said, 'I don't want my mama and sister to know I have failed.'

The lads hadn't messed about taking Piotr under their wing and telling him to pack his things because they weren't getting back to their mother-in-law that they'd left him living in squalor. Piotr had come to stay in room one of the guesthouse for a few nights, becoming acquainted with the little red fox and Mrs Flaherty's fry-ups. Quinn decided to give him a go in the kitchen of his bistro and reckoned Piotr, under his watchful eye, had the making of a good sous chef. Things had a way of working out and Paula, one of the waitresses employed at Quinn's, had a friend looking for someone to rent a room in the flat she'd taken a lease out on. Piotr's new wage meant it was within reach. He was even managing to send money home.

Tomasina said she owed Maureen everything and had gifted her with Polish treats, too, but Maureen said that was nonsense. It was just what you did when you were working on a cruise ship and had become one big family.

Speaking of which . . .

'There they are!' Maureen cried, waving out.

The End.

A Letter from Michelle Vernal

♥

Dear Lovely Reader,

Thank you for picking up *Cruising with the O'Maras*, Book 17 in the *Irish Guesthouse on the Green* series. I hope the story whisked you away on a little holiday—minus the tequila and ping-pong shenanigans, of course! I also hope it made you giggle as much as I do while writing about this family and their escapades.

There are plenty more O'Mara stories to come! I can't wait to explore what's next aboard the Mayan Princess when the rest of the family joins Maureen and Donal. Oh, and I'm curious how things work out for Carole and Tomasina, too, with their complicated personal lives; how about you? I'd love to hear your thoughts!

To explain why there's no pre-order link for Book 18, it's because 2025 will be a hectic year on the writing front. At the moment, I don't have a scheduled publication date, but I promise you more O'Mara stories are on their way.

If you'd like to keep up with the O'Maras and my latest releases, you can sign up for my newsletter via www.mich

A LETTER FROM MICHELLE VERNAL

ellevernalbooks.com. Rest assured, your email address will remain private, and you can unsubscribe anytime.

If you enjoyed this story, it would mean the world to me if you left a review. Your feedback not only helps me but also makes it easier for new readers to discover my books—thank you so much!

Finally, if you feel part of this madcap Irish family, I think you'll adore the Kellys of Emerald Bay in my *Little Irish Village* stories. Plus, I'm super-excited to announce a brand-new series, *The Irish Adoption House*, coming later this year!

I love hearing from my readers, so feel free to reach out to me on my Facebook page or through my website.

www.facebook.com/michellevernalnovelist
www.michellevernalbooks.com/
xx Michelle

Printed in Great Britain
by Amazon